No
Country
For
Young
Fools

No Country
For
Young
Fools

Sidonie Walsh

XULON PRESS

Xulon Press
2301 Lucien Way #415
Maitland, FL 32751
407.339.4217
www.xulonpress.com

Printed in the United States of America.

ISBN-13: 978-1-5456-7793-3

You are my refuge and my shield; Your word is my source of **hope**.
<u>Psalm 119:114</u> <u>NLT</u>

Dedication

I dedicate this book to my Circle. God in the center of it—illuminating life, love and hope. Where the resounding vibrations of others rotate and push me forward. Chances are you are a part of it—whether bringing a buzz, a breeze or a scream—all adding sound, purpose and movement to my journey.

Table of Contents

Prologue

What if someone brought you into a room, sat you down, and told you that everything you knew as true was now false? What if the values you'd held all your life were no more? What if the people who you felt sure you knew decided to change one day?

That's exactly how I felt when my father left my life. It felt like someone telling me that the grass, which I'd always known to be green, was now red. That the sky, once blue, was now gray.

My father, Sheldon Ellis, had been a renowned journalist in Jamaica. He wrote several of the island's bestselling books on politics, corruption, and gang matriculation. He was the face of journalism, one of the professionals who informed everyone of the island's current events. He would watch TV while talking, but, when the news came on, he would stop in midsentence, almost mesmerized, bothered by the things he saw.

Though he didn't say much, I could almost see his brain collecting and compartmentalizing information, then deciding what he would do. I used to wonder what he was thinking, but I never made a sound or let him know that I observed his every move. He was always doing research on the computer, circling what people said in the newspaper, and leaving handwritten notes on various topics laying around. Even in the middle of the night, when everyone was fast asleep, he was downstairs, typing away. With his glasses on and his cup of coffee next to him, he got in the zone, power typing with sparks in his eyes. He would do this for several months straight, then he would have a manuscript, and, suddenly, a book!

And so it went. Eight manuscripts later, schools on the island used his books. Although he's been gone for years, I can't help feeling that disappearing wasn't a part of his plan. This was not supposed to happen.

Still, it's hard for me to take anything seriously; nothing lasts forever. Why build relationships? Why get passionate? Why commit to anything or anyone? I don't. Everything that I consider real can be yanked from under me at any given moment.

Chapter 1

Summer in the country

saw them getting smaller in the distance. I stuck my head out the window and waved goodbye as my mother pulled away, driving me home.

"I'll miss you guys!" I yelled.

Everyone stood by the gate and waved except Sam and Jeff, who ran behind the car. They kept up until they, too, faded from sight as we reached the end of the gravel road and turned onto the main street.

I had spent the first month of my summer vacation at my grandparents' farmhouse. I dreaded it at first, wondering what I would do each day, but I have to admit it wasn't so bad. It's funny how little everyday things can become such events.

Their majestic farmhouse sat on top of a hill bordered by a white picket fence. Willow trees and bamboo plants, swaying in the gentle wind, lined the long, winding road towards the house. We filled the farmhouse's five bedrooms to capacity.

I had a daily routine. I would wake up at five-thirty in the morning to sit on the veranda with my mint tea in hand. The mint grew in Grandma Lilith's garden and its aroma would wake up my senses. I'd sit there for about an hour, just looking at the mountains. My eyes would follow the mountain's peak in admiration, up to where it hid within a cluster of clouds. With my feet folded under each other and the dawn about to break, I'd close my eyes and take time to reflect on life and God's wondrous artwork.

It almost felt like a mystical experience. My body light and my mind clear, I'd drift into deep meditation. I felt closer to my Creator than ever. The rooster crowed. The potent smell of the smoke from the neighbor's wood fire filled the air. I soaked it all up, taking deep breaths.

All my worries and insecurities in life ceased. I had no anxiety or panic attacks. There would be no, "Morgan, push past the clutter and focus on what it is that you want." In the country, I felt like the world was there for the taking. I could breathe without asking my heart to slow down. Eventually, I'd hear everyone else in the house waking up and I'd jump to my feet, empowered to start the day.

Every morning in the country, my cousins and I moved the cows to greener pastures, fed the chickens, cleaned the pigsty, and started breakfast. We would send Sam and Jeff under the cellar where the chickens hide out to collect eggs for breakfast. Ann and I were tasked with making fried dumplings and coffee. When the meal was ready, we would sit on the benches around their big dining table that I was convinced could hold twenty people.

Ann always made the fried dumplings—perfectly round and as big as a tennis ball. Biting into the golden-brown crust with the perfect hint of sweetness made it hard to resist a second and—for Uncle Mack—a third! I tried to make them a few times, but to no avail. Mine came out either chewy or burnt outside and undercooked inside—and never as big. After my second attempt, my grandpa kindly complimented me on my coffee and suggested Ann stick to making the dumplings.

Bathing created a hassle every morning. Nine people sharing one bathroom left us no choice but to enforce a time limit—ten minutes per person.

"No more, no less," said Grandma Lilith.

"No less?" I asked her, thinking that should not be a problem.

She leaned in close and said in her usual humorous tone, "If I left it to Sam and Jeff, they would get wet and out the tub in thirty seconds flat."

I laughed at that.

We would each jump in the white cast-iron bathtub, embracing the cold water under the pipe. Having no showerhead made it inconvenient, to say the least. I would curl into an almost fetal position to wash the soap off my back.

My cousin Deon always took more time than allowed. We would stand outside the bathroom door, yelling constantly, "Deon, hurry up!" No matter how annoyed we got, she was the eldest and we had to accept it.

Within two hours, we would be dressed to face the world. Our days consisted of a lot of walking. We walked everywhere on the red dirt and gravel streets, which were rough on my shoes. After the first two days, I learned to wear my least favorite ones to save the others. We would walk our usual routes to Ms. Icy shop to get groceries or up the road to bring neighbors food from my Grandpa's garden, and to church. We went to church a lot.

"We go church four days a week," Ann explained when I first got there. It took me some time to get use to her strong accent and word omissions. Of course, she and my other cousins teased me about how I "twanged" all the time. At my school in Kingston, we had our Jamaican accents, but they insisted that we speak the Queen's English. Each word that we spoke was expected to be well-enunciated and free from patois. In the country, though, it seemed like they had another dialect altogether.

"Sunday school start ten and church eleven-thirty til tree pan Sunday," she said.

I always wanted to correct her and say, "You mean three on Sundays, right?" But I always just smiled and nodded instead.

"Afta dat we go home fi eat dinna and go back a church seven til ten."

"Why don't we just stay there all day?" I'd asked her.

4

She just smiled and said, in the coarsest way that I've ever heard my name pronounced, "Margan? Mi a ask da question deh fi years."

After our morning routine, I'd usually be no use to myself on Mondays; I got off to a slow start. Bible study came on Wednesdays, then youth meeting on Fridays, and sometimes we had to follow my grandmother for choir rehearsals on Saturdays.

At one youth meeting, I remember thinking, *This isn't so bad.* They were discussing the proper way for young women to dress. I, for the most part, agreed. I dressed conservatively. Then they took it to another level.

A short bald man on the discussion panel boldly announced, "Women skin should not be shown except the skin on her face."

I laughed to myself as I looked down at my short-sleeved top and knee-length skirt. I must be committing the worst sin in his eyes, but leave it to a man to come up with such theory. I thought this was crazy talk, especially living on an island with an average temperature of 90 degrees a day. The warm sea breeze provided the only air-conditioning in most homes here.

On another occasion, an old lady down the street, Ms. Pincy, saw me and my two cousins, Precious and Ann, walking to church in sleeveless dresses and boldly proclaimed, "Bout unu a go church, a man unu want!"

That comment shocked me because there were absolutely no men worth looking at in church. Most of them, old, disgusting and smelly, looked like they had spent their entire lives drinking, then decided to give church a try in their old age. They were dispassionate and crass, like the unattractive old women by their sides. They didn't make Christianity look appealing. I thought a sinner would want to stay away from whatever made them the way they were. In their own minds, though, they were holier than thou. They knew how to quote the Bible–even if they seemed miserable and unconvinced.

One woman turned up her nose at me and told me if I wanted to go to heaven, I should first take the earrings out of my ears. I like natural beauty–less is more. However, common sense told me that taking out my earrings had nothing to do with me going to heaven. I smiled at her, then slowly walked away.

When there was no church, we lived outdoors. We would sit under the coconut tree and play board games, hopscotch, and Chinese skip all day, while my grandfather picked coconuts to keep us refreshed.

At about four o' clock, we would stop whatever we were doing to collect wood to make the fire in preparation for dinner. Ann and I had cleaning duty after dinner most of the time. Sam and Jeff were responsible for getting the fire going. Precious, Deon, my Grandpa Sonny loved to cook, so they happily volunteered to do it.

During the summer, Grandpa Sonny walked around calling Grandma Lilith the queen. She got to sit back and relax while we took care of her regular affairs. After dinner, Grandpa would entertain us with stories of how he met Grandma Lilith and how she played hard to get. He told those stories well, but I must say that ghost stories were his forte. He did everything he could to scare us with local sightings that I knew he made up on the spot.

Then we would watch the news, since my grandparents only got the two main national stations, TVJ and CVM. The only thing on the news that applied locally was that the farmers were demanding more money for their crops.

"We wuk too hard fi give weh wi crops fi likkle or nuttin!" one man exclaimed.

"How mi a go feed mi family if mi give weh mi livelihood?" another said.

Everything else focused on the crime and violence in Kingston. Election year had come and the two parties, the People's National Party and the Jamaica Labour Party, were holding rallies all over the island. On the TV, we saw people making their choice known by wearing the colors of their parties. People supporting JLP wore green and the PNP filled the road with orange. Back home in Kingston, ordinary people had to be careful what they wore to make sure they would not be thrown in with a party.

I appreciated the changes in my life that came from staying in the country. God knows I would not be able to see such wonderful scenery and be so relaxed back at home. Yet I still felt a little excited to go home when the time came.

Chapter 2

August

The lush greenery and the bright blooms on the trees rushed past me as I stared out the window. I tried to count the trees as we passed them, but Roxann drove too fast. I lost count at sixty-two. I had diagnosed myself with a mild case of OCD. For as long as I could remember, I had always felt the need to count every-thing—the number of blocks on the sidewalk, the thir-teen stairs to get to my room, and the number of trees I passed on the road.

I pushed my head out slightly to feel the stinging brush of the warm, clean breeze against my face. My best friend Peyton had written me several letters while I was in the country, since my grandparents' home had no phone reception. She missed me and told me that, because I was gone, she was bored out of her mind. In her last letter, she had even said she was going to try Jesus. Just the thought of that high ambition made me chuckle. Free-spirited Peyton didn't have the attention span for church or anything that involved her commit-ting to anything or anyone.

"What's so funny?" asked Roxann.

"Nothing," I lied. "I'm just really happy to go home."

"I thought you would miss the country," Roxann said, looking at me curiously. "Grandma Lilith said that you fit right in and so happy every day; I almost didn't want to come for you."

I knew she had suggested me going there in the first place because I had no life at home. I couldn't keep up with Peyton, who changed her interests in people, music, and styles at the drop of a hat. Roxann called me the responsible one, especially when comparing me to my older brother, Anthony. I went to school, worked in her store, and went home. I didn't have a lot of friends, but Anthony was quite the opposite, almost like Peyton.

I've always been called an old soul, though. I have never really been interested in being reckless like other teenagers. I didn't judge them—actually, I secretly admired their willingness to venture into the unknown and come out with even just a piece of it. For now, though, it was enough for me to live vicariously through them.

"I will miss the country, but it's still nice to be going home," I finally said to her.

I woke up the next morning to my mother and brother talking about the election and all the crazy things happening in the streets. Roxann worried about driving through Half-Way-Tree, where the rallies would be.

"Tony, I won't make it to work in time–or alive, for that matter—if I drive through there," Roxann complained.

I heard my brother giving her directions to a back road that would get her to her store. We had to drive through the town of Half-Way-Tree to get around most times. With all the rallies, we would have to be careful. That didn't sit well with Roxann, who was a busy woman. She owned a clothing store in New Kingston and was scouting locations to open up another store. She kept her days filled with appointments, so she worried how she would get around without being delayed by the rallies.

I stayed in bed a little longer. My room had a weird scent, which I guessed to be a mixture of paint and vanilla bean air freshener. Roxann had called me while I was in the country and asked me to choose between brown and blue for a room color.

"I guess brown, but only on one wall," I had told her.

I got exactly that, but with all her extra trimmings. I now had fancy champagne-colored drapes pulled to one side with brown tassels. A new glass desk graced one corner of my room, facing the window that overlooked the fountain on our well-manicured lawn. *Talk about an environment conducive to learning,* I thought. All through high school, I had used the computer downstairs, but now that I was starting college, Roxann thought I should have one in my room.

A cozy seat with yellow and green cushions sat under the other window. Everything seems so quiet and organized. After a few minutes, I was up on my feet heading to the shower. I went downstairs dressed in a bright green wrap top—one of Roxann's great creations—and beige capris. I completed my outfit with a neat ponytail, my small beige heels, and brown and green accessories.

As I came around the bend into the kitchen, my brother fell silent, a puzzled look coming over his face.

"Now why would you decide to wear a big bright green blouse at a time when people are killing over these things?"

"Good morning to you, too, Tony."

"Morgan Lee, you have to be conscious of your surroundings. Haven't you been watching the news?" Roxann scolded. I knew she had to be serious when she called me by my first and middle name.

"Two people were shot on Monday just for wearing the wrong colors on the wrong side of town."

"Wow—I saw tidbits here and there on the news in the country, but I had no idea it was this bad."

"Be careful while you are driving, too," Tony chimed in. "Go on the road only if necessary."

I understood their concerns, but, since I'd been in the country, the outdoors had become my haven. They were not going to be able to keep me in the house today.

I had two more weeks before my first day as a college student and I knew I had some catching up to do with Peyton. After changing out of the green blouse, I went downstairs wearing my most inoffensive white shirt. Roxann was still mapping out a driving route. I waved to her and Tony.

"I'll be safe, I promise. I'm just driving around the road to Peyton's house."

It felt good to be driving again. I had not driven my car during my exile in the country. Actually, I hadn't been driving it for very long before that. Roxann had recently upgraded to a new car and had given me her Honda Accord, that was only three years old, as an early graduation gift.

At first, I had been reluctant to take the car. I have always had a thing about my independence. I knew that the minute she was not happy with me, Roxann would want to put restrictions on using the car. In the end, though, she'd convinced me to take the car as payment for all the weekends and late evenings I had worked at her store.

I do deserve this, I thought as I drove to Peyton's house.

She was already outside waiting for me when I pulled up a few minutes later.

"Oh my God, you're really back!" she screamed as she yanked me out of the car, hugging me excitedly.

"Okay, okay! I was only gone a month," I said, closing the door.

"It was not a month," she carried on. "It was a month and two days, but who's counting?"

"You look great–I love the new do!" Her short, spiky haircut had red and gold highlights that shone bright in the sun. She opened the door to her house and a delicious smell floated out. I walked through the living room to the kitchen where, sure enough, Peyton's mom was cooking up a storm.

"Hi, Aunty Madge," I said, giving her a big hug.

"We really missed you around here, Morgan. It's so good to have you back. Peyton has been out and about making new friends while you were gone."

"Out of sight, out of mind, I guess. New friends, huh?" I nudged Peyton.

"Oh, please. Don't listen to Mommy; she's just making stuff up." She pushed me out of the kitchen toward her room.

"You'll stay for lunch, right, Morgan?" Aunty Madge yelled after me.

"Wouldn't miss it," I called back.

Like Peyton, her room had been through renovations. The bed now slanted across the right corner of the room, covered by a beautiful purple and green comforter with an assortment of cushions. Her walls were devoid of all the boy band posters that used to be her backdrop and an elegant striped rug covered the floor.

"Nice," I said. "Someone's been busy."

"Tell me about it," she said. "My sister was in town two weeks ago and insisted that my room needed a makeover."

"What's with them? Mommy did an overhaul in my room, too." I moved over to her mirror and saw a picture of Peyton hugging a good-looking guy that I did not recognize.

"Ooh, and who do we have here?"

"Oh, that's just Eric," she said guiltily as she smiled from ear to ear.

"And who is this Eric and how did he make it onto your mirror? You've been holding out on me. Is this the new friend that Aunty Madge mentioned?"

"No, she is talking about everyone, not him in particular."

"Everyone, huh?"

"That's not what I mean!" she yelled, then attempted to explain. "After you left for the summer, I was bored most of the time. I mean, other than working at the salon I didn't do much. Mommy saw some kids going to that church on the corner on Friday nights and said I should check it out. I went the next Friday and found out they turn the church in a club! I mean, disco ball, dancing, and all. I walked in and thought I was at the wrong place. When I turned to leave, I bumped into a tall, red-boned boy who held me up. He said, 'Slow down, nice girl,' as he helped me get my balance. So I apologized and asked him if he knew where the church was around here. He laughed and told me that I was at the right place, but they started their meetings this way, praising and worshipping like it was a club to appeal to young people. I've been hanging out with him and some of his friends recently, but it's still too soon to put a label on it. We are just friends!"

"Just friends? Oh, it makes sense now. So this is what you mean by trying Jesus? Interesting…," I said, laughing.

"So enough about me," she changed the subject. "Tell me about the country. I'm sure it was awful. I mean, when I felt sorry for myself, I imagined what you must have been going through."

I smiled. "The country was fine—actually, it was better than fine. I now have a new appreciation for the outdoors, church, walking, cows, pigs, and…."

"And what?" she asked.

"Oh nothing."

"And what?" she insisted.

"Okay, okay … and love," I finally said.

"Morgan Lee Ellis," she exclaimed. "You're talking about me; look at you! No wonder you loved the country so much. You found a man. Who is he?"

By then I was laughing. "Who is who? You are way out in left field— my appreciation for love has nothing to do with a guy. It's just inspiration from Grandpa Sonny and Grandma Lilith. They have been married for forty-nine years—seeing them together and hearing their stories of how they met and their life together kind of had me thinking…you know?"

Peyton busted out laughing. "You are kidding me, right? What did you do with my best friend? This cannot be coming from the same person who said that she would never get married, the one who has turned down every guy who has approached her since second form. No, this can't be; I have to see this for myself. Did I tell you that Eric has some cute friends? You have to come to church with me this weekend."

The bell chimed on the door of Roxann's store. She had me working at the store today while she brought Lisa, her only worker, with her to scout models for her upcoming fall fashion show. I had helped a few customers earlier, but the store had been empty until now. A heavyset woman walked in, looking around the store.

"Good morning. Welcome to Lee's! I'm Morgan; can I help you find something?"

"Let's hope so," she said walking closer to me. "I'm looking for an outfit for an art exhibit and dinner that I have tonight. I've been looking all week and still nothing."

"No worries, you've come to the right place," I lied.

I wasn't even sure if my mom carried anything in her size. My mother's usual clients tend to be thin, stylish, young professionals. This lady looked like maybe a size eighteen and she wore frumpy clothes.

"Ah…give me just a second and I'll see what I can find," I told her.

Few minutes later, I brought back a black cocktail dress with silver trimming on the front as well as a pair of tan pants with a brown and orange chiffon top. She looked unsure as I approached.

"You're about a size eighteen, right?" I asked.

"I'm not even sure," she said hesitantly.

"Okay. Well, I found two things that I think would be perfect for the occasion. This black dress is a size sixteen, but I think it is cut well for you and you cannot go wrong with a little black dress."

She smiled when I said that.

"The pants and top are size eighteen. The colors will be perfect for the summer," I added.

"Okay, I'll try them," she said.

Ten minutes later, she still had not come out, so I went by the door to check on her. "How is everything working out in there?"

"Everything is fine; I'll be out soon," she said.

"No problem. Let me know if there is anything that I can get for you."

A few minutes later she came out with both outfits in her hands. I had thought she would show me the outfits before taking them off. Since she hadn't, I felt sure she didn't like them.

She came over to the register and said, "I'll take them both."

"Wow, I'm so happy you liked them."

"They are perfect. I'll wear the pants and top tonight, then save the dress for the holidays. As you said, you can't go wrong with a little black dress—plus, I could lose about five pounds and it will fit like a glove."

I rang her up and handed her the bags. "You have a great day. And have fun tonight—you will look fabulous!"

"You know, Ms. Morgan, you have a true gift for fashion. If your boss were here, I would tell her you need a raise. Thank you so much for all your help; you cannot begin to imagine how grateful I am."

As she was leaving, she turned around and said, "You know, my husband and I are pastors at the church at the corner of Norbrook Road and 7th Street. I would love if you could come by to our youth meeting tomorrow night."

I smiled at her as she handed me her business card. *Bonnie Davis, Pastor, Oasis Ministries.*

Peyton would be pleased; now I had two invitations to the same church on Friday night.

Before long, business at Lee's was booming again. By lunchtime, I could have killed my mom for leaving me there all by myself. One lady wanted my opinion on all seven outfits that she tried on. She countered every opinion I gave her with a negative question.

"But don't you think it's too big at the back?" she'd say.

Three other ladies came from the bank in the same plaza. They were rushing to get back to work before their lunch hour ended. I rang them up while giving a thumbs-up to customers coming out of the dressing room as well as greeting customers as they came in. The door chime rang again; a guy in a green shirt with orange writing walked into the store. He wore a red bandana and dark glasses and stood by the door surveying the room like he was looking for something.

"Good afternoon; welcome to Lee's," I said.

He didn't acknowledge me—or maybe he didn't hear me over all the chattering in the store. He just backed up quickly, gave me a slight glance, and he walked out.

"Have a nice—" I began, but he was already gone. *How rude*. I snapped back to reality and gave one of the bank ladies her change.

By the time my mom and Lisa came back, it was already five o'clock. Due to all the violence, Roxann had decided to close the store at six o'clock for the next few weeks, until the election. Before she had left, she promised me that she would be back by three, but Roxann was always on Jamaican time, so I can't say I was surprised.

She brought me some jerk chicken from Red Hills Road, which helped with my fatigue since hunger definitely made it worse. By now, the store was calm compared to lunchtime. One woman browsed while two others tried on clothes in the fitting room.

Lisa quickly took over as she came in.

I went in the break room to eat while I watched the five o'clock news on CVM.

The election rallies were still in full swing. The reporter, Rachel Lawson, reported more uproar over the upcoming election.

"Two men in Waterhouse stabbed each other while engaged in a heated discussion about the party better suited to handle the state of the country. Both men were rushed to Kingston Public Hospital, where one is listed in critical condition. In a press conference today at Jamaica House, Prime Minister Desmond Porter urged everyone to refrain from violence and to keep the peace," she reported before a sound bite from the Prime Minister played.

"Election should be a time when we put our differences aside and do what's best for the country," said Desmond Porter. *"Different viewpoints should not be met with violence, but with respect and an appreciation that we live in a country that gives us the freedom to*

choose our leaders. Jamaican citizens should feel safe regardless of their views and there will be no tolerance for those who refuse to uphold the law. You should not resort to violence, but remember to live up to our motto, 'out of many, one people'," Porter finished.

I could hear Roxann in the store raving to Lisa on how much I had sold today as she straightened the clothes on the racks. She knew every piece in the store; after all, she had designed and made most of them.

"What happened to that black dress?" she asked.

"Sold!" I shouted.

"You are good," she said, appearing in the break room. "You know how long I've had that dress with no takers?"

"I really didn't do much; you're the one who made the dress. I had a plus-size customer and I had no choice but to offer her what we had. By the way, she really liked your designs, so you might want to expand your size selections."

"Look at all the worthless people marching on the road!" Roxann exclaimed as she looked up at the news. "Some of them don't even know why they're marching. They need to go work like the rest of us. You know the majority of them live in the ghetto and they are only voting for the party who bribed and promised them the most handouts. I work hard to pay my bills, while they march and kill and get their light and water bills paid."

That's when I saw him again. Sure enough, the camera zoomed in on the guy in the orange and green shirt on the screen, walking along with the no-income ghetto people. My heart dropped.

"Oh my God, that's the guy!" I yelled.

"What guy?" Roxann asked.

"That one to the side in the two-colored shirt. He was the rude guy who was in here today," I said, still in shock.

"He was in my store? Lee's? Today? Why?" Roxann asked, confused.

I shook my head. "I don't know. He just came in, stood at the door, and looked around. I greeted him, but he just left without saying a word."

"This is serious," Roxann said as she called Lisa in the breakroom to fill her in. "They are taking over. Now they are coming into my store, which they definitely have no business in. If he or any of them come by again while either of you are here, call the police! I might have to close Lee's even earlier and see if Tony can stay here some days, too, so no one is ever in the store alone."

I had not seen my mother this worried in a long time. *Is all this real?* The severity of the time hit me full on. Suddenly I just wanted to be home.

Chapter 3

I woke up to the sound of rain against my window on Friday morning. My room was even darker than usual as heavy clouds blocked the sun. The house still and quiet; I figured my mom and Tony were still asleep. The pounding rain made it so peaceful in the dark.

I rested, deep in thought. In two weeks, I would be at the University of the West Indies, studying God knows what. I was leaning towards journalism. When I was younger, I used to watch CNN. I would see the journalists on the frontline, reporting the news as it happened all around the world. I wanted to do that. I wanted to be the voice of a nation. I wanted to go and dig out the stories that affected humanity and bring them to light.

Somewhere along the way–maybe in high school—I had lost my passion. It might have been because the guidance counselor, Mr. Burgess, told me that I would have to establish myself before I can make any money.

"Journalists are all flukes. They tell the news they want to tell and not the truth. People don't read anymore, anyway. That's good because journalists have lost their credibility," he said.

Thank you for killing my dreams, Mr. Burgess. My mother wanted me to study business. "You can't go wrong with business, Morgan," she'd say. "You may even be able to take over the store one day."

I finally decided to enroll as an undecided student, so I could figure it out as I go. I wasn't sure, though. Being undecided felt just like that...undecided. Nothing was clear.

I wished I could be like Peyton, who had known she wanted to be a hair stylist for as long as I could remember. She had gone to cosmetology school in the evenings while still in high school. She would have her cosmetology license by Christmas and would do a business program at U-Tech next year, in hopes of owning her own salon one day. It seemed a lot more comfortable to be on solid ground than to try to balance on the fence.

Dazed and thoughtful, I went over to my window seat and curled up with my hands over my knees. I remembered Grandma Lilith telling me to pray when I felt uncertain about what I wanted to do with my life.

"Prayer changes things," she'd say.

So I tried it for the first in a long time. I looked out into the rain, undecided, open to whatever may come, and I prayed. I asked for passion, clarity, decisiveness, and happiness. The rain stopped right on cue; the sun snuck through the clouds and lit my room. I took that illumination and calm as God's response, assuring me that everything would be just fine.

"No, you cannot cut my hair!" I said to Peyton as she tried to convince me to do one of her infamous makeovers.

On weekends, Peyton washed hair at Trends, the top salon in town. She had insisted that I come over to get my hair done before I start my new life as a college student. But I knew she really wanted me to look good for church that night. It was not busy yet. Peyton, her boss Ange, and a hairstylist named Sharon were the only ones in the salon and the other two both had customers. Two people who wanted cornrows waited for Shay, the natural hairstylist who worked the afternoon shift. She was due into work any minute. I was relieved to be there before the normal Friday afternoon crowd of women getting ready for the weekend.

"Okay," Peyton said. "How about we make a deal?"

"What deal?"

"If you let me cut your hair—"

"You are not going to cut my hair!"

"Will you just listen?" she continued. "If you don't let me cut your hair, I will tell Eric to have his friend Bones ask you out."

"Bones—what kind of name is that?"

"Oh, so all you're worried about is his name. Wait till you meet him, you are going to wish you had made me cut your hair," she teased.

"Okay, I am not interested in meeting Bones—or anyone else for that matter. How about you create an illusion?" I suggested.

"An illusion?"

"Yes, give me a style that creates the illusion that I cut my hair."

I had been growing my hair since I was in the fifth grade. I was not about to give in so easily.

"It's a deal, but I have to be able to do whatever I want to do without any interruptions."

"Alright then, go ahead. You won't hear a peep out of me.

Three hours later, Peyton and I were back at my house, in my room, trying to find outfits for tonight. Having Roxann as my mother had its perks; her talent and fabulous fashion sense made my closet a young girl's dream. First of all, there was the actual closet. A few years ago, Roxann had a professional closet company come in to put custom, built-in shelving in all the closets in the house.

Then came the clothes. Roxann believed that every young lady should have all assortments of clothes and styles to choose from. I had fashion for every occasion, even those that I would never attend. I had a variety of culture wraps, countless dresses for the beach, long flowing gowns for a ball, skirts in every length and styles. Everything was unusual and stylish due to my mom's vivid imagination.

"Oh, I love this," said Peyton, from deep in the section of my closet that I call the unmentionables.

That section holds those clothes that I've never worn and will never wear. They stay there for my mother's peace of mind—and for Peyton. None of them fit my conservative and basic style.

Peyton, on the other hand, pushed the envelope. She always had on something that I would never wear, like miniskirts and shorts with rips in all the wrong places, flashy belts and swanky boots. She wore way too much jewelry and makeup, and she had a funky, edgy hairstyle for every season in her life. For some reason, my mother had put clothes like that in my closet and only Peyton wore them.

"Who needs to go to the mall when I can come here and shop for free?" she said now.

She came out the closet in a red leather skirt that actually went to her knees, paired with a fitted black top.

"Wow, that skirt actually reaches your knees," I said, smiling.

"Well, after all, I am going to church," she replied.

I lay on the bed, trying not to mess up my hair that Peyton worked so hard on. After she put what seemed like a hundred rollers in my hair and stuck me under the dryer for an hour and a half, she and the ladies in the salon had brought out a mirror to show me the big reveal. I have to say I was pleasantly surprised.

"Great illusion," I said, smiling and admiring my new do.

Peyton had looked very pleased with herself. My hair, now fluffy with curls, bounced as it barely touched my shoulders. If I didn't know better, I would have thought I actually did get a haircut. It gave my face a new glow and, I must admit, it lifted my spirits, too.

I heard sounds from downstairs; Tony was on his phone in the kitchen. He was working for my mother today, unloading fabric into her sewing room. Tony calls himself an entrepreneur. Two years ago, after he'd tried college and decided it wasn't for him, he and two of his friends, Ronnie and Flex, started a car upgrade business. They would take even the worst of cars and transform them into something unique. They gave the cars fresh paint jobs and tricked out interiors. In some cars, they installed televisions, high-end stereos, and personalized seats and dashboards. *Your wish is our command*, the slogan for their company, was written all over their cars. Now and then, he also helped Roxann with her business, picking up fabrics and clothes when they come in from the Wharf. I guessed he didn't have a choice in the matter; after all, he was the man of the house.

Tony hadn't always been this together, so, by sheer contrast, I had been labeled the responsible one. In high school, he had hung out with the wrong crowd and gotten in trouble constantly. At sixteen, he had been kicked out of two high schools and barely graduated from the last one. Through a contact Roxann had at the local trade school, he had explored his artistic talents. He had a true gift for drawing and painting, but he had other plans and got caught up with the wrong crowd again. One night he was caught stealing a car and had to do some jail time. It was only thirty days, but Roxann said it was the best thing that ever could have happened to him. He obviously loved cars, so he found a trade school that taught him how to fix them and use his art to create designs. He met Ronnie and Flex there and the rest was history.

Downstairs, I could hear him making plans to go to Quad tonight. A nightclub in town, Quad was where all the kids in high school wanted to go, but were too young to go. They had to know someone there to get in. Right now, Tony sounded persuasive and proper, so I knew he was talking to a girl. He had never introduced us to the girls that he dated. On occasion, when he would stop by the house to pick up something, I would look out the kitchen window and see a girl in his car. I had never seen the same one twice and he had never invited any of them inside.

"Tony, why don't you invite your friend inside?" my mom would ask.

"I'm only stopping for a minute," he'd say.

But I knew better. He had once told me that he'd only invite a girl inside if she was someone special. I guess he had not found that person yet.

"Morgan." I heard someone calling my name.

"Yes…yes, what is it?" I mumbled sleepily.

It was Tony. "I thought you and Peyton had some-where to go tonight."

"We do. We're going to the church down the road. Wait a minute—what time is it? And where is Peyton?" I asked him.

"It's seven and I guess Peyton went home," he answered.

"She was in the closet earlier, trying on clothes," I said, confused.

He walked into the closet and chuckled. Sure enough, Peyton was in there, fast asleep on top of some clothes. He lifted her up and brought her into the room. She still had on my red leather skirt, now stuck to her skin, and she was knocked out. I started laughing and she woke up enough to hang her hand around Tony's neck. He looked at her intently, a strange but admiring look on his face.

For the longest time, I used to think that they liked each other. In high school, Peyton had always acted weirdly mature around him and she had gotten a bad attitude whenever I told her about his many girls. Plus, she insisted on calling him Anthony no matter how much I corrected her; she said she liked Anthony better.

He, on the other hand, never pulled any punches with me, yet when it came to Peyton, he turned soft and charming. I saw a glimmer on his face as he looked at her sleeping and wondered if I was missing some piece of information. She never said anything about liking him and neither had he. They both dated other people, so I might have been crazy and reading too much into things.

As he placed her carefully next to me on the bed, she woke up, confused. She looked at me, then at him.

"What's going on?" she asked.

"We fell asleep," I told her.

"And you fell asleep in the closet," Tony added.

She started to laugh. "Shopping can be such hard work. Oh, wait—what time is it?"

"It's after seven," Tony told her.

"Oh my God, Morgan, we have to get dressed! I told Eric we would meet him outside the church at 7:30."

She jumped to her feet, pushing Tony out the door. His expression dimmed as he went through the door. Before she closed the door, she stopped. "Oh, Anthony... thanks for picking me up."

There was silence. She looked out the door at him with the same glimmering look that he had given her earlier.

"No worries," he said.

She closed the door so we could get dressed and I knew for sure that I wasn't crazy.

We pulled up to the Oasis at 7:45. There was one girl walking into the church and things seemed to be in full swing on the inside.

"No Eric, huh?" I asked.

"I guess he had to go inside," she said, still looking around for him.

We walked towards the door, me in my navy and white wrap dress with some red wedges and Peyton in her red leather skirt with a black top, gold belt, and black boots, accented by black eye-shadow, mascara, and black and red accessories. She looked striking. I had to admire her; for some reason, the excess worked for her.

We heard the faint music from inside as we got closer to the door. We opened the door and a loud blast of music and lights met us at the door.

"Oh my God, this is crazy!" I shouted to Peyton.

"Isn't it?" she said, smiling.

The dark room with disco lights bouncing from wall to wall was packed with at least a hundred young teen-agers jumping up and down. An older guy and three young women led the party on the stage, along with a pianist, drummer, and guitarist. Just then, they stopped singing and turned the microphone to the crowd as they chanted the chorus to the song on the screen:

You must fight, be brave against all evil
Never run, nor even lag behind
If you would win for God and the right
Just keep on the firin' line

They kept chanting, *Fight, be brave; Fight be brave,* and then the music started up again.

Peyton and I snuck behind the crowd to some seats in the back. "Okay, I admit that this is different!" I shouted over the music.

Peyton smiled at me as she bounced to the music.

"Do they do this all night?" I asked.

"No, you'll see," she said reassuringly.

A guy walked through the door carrying two cases of sodas toward the kitchen. Still trying to get over my initial shock and get comfortable, I got up to open the kitchen door for him. He kept his eyes forward and barely said thank you. *Okay, then.* I sat back down next to bouncing Peyton, who was scouring the room, unaware that I had even gotten up.

"Oh, there he is," she finally said as three guys from the crowd walked towards us.

She jumped up. "Come on, Morgan!"

I wanted to ask, *For what*? Instead, I just stayed seated. She met them, hugging a tall, light-skinned guy who I assumed to be redboned Eric. They started talking, then beckoned me over. Eventually they came to where I was sitting.

"Morgan, meet Eric, Lamb, and Bones!" she shouted. "Guys, this is my best friend, Morgan."

They waved. Eric put his hand out and said, "Very nice to finally meet you. Peyton hasn't stopped talking about you."

"Good things, I hope," I said, giving him my best fake smile.

"Well, of course."

Fifteen minutes passed, the music mellowed, and everyone lifted their hands up in worship, including Peyton. Eric convinced her to go out onto the floor. I respectfully declined when invited; I sat still, observing this new switch. Some people lay on the floor, praying while they worshiped. I started to think of my own issues and a feeling of anxiety came over me. I closed my eyes as they sang, trying to meditate and to focus on positive thoughts. The words of the song rang through my head as I got lost in my own worship and entered in.

> *Bow down and worship Him, enter in, oh enter in*
> *Bow down and worship Him, enter in, oh enter in*
> *Consuming fire, sweet perfume*
> *Your awesome presence fills this room*
> *This is holy ground, this is holy ground*
> *So, come and bow, bow down*

I opened my eyes with the music still playing in the background and the weirdest thing happened. The guy who had carried the soda into the kitchen earlier was leaning on the back wall, just staring at me. A sudden flush came over me and I turned away. After a few seconds, I glanced back at him; this time he was looking into the crowd. Something felt oddly familiar about him.

The lights came on; the room looked like a new place now that I could see all of it. Chairs were stacked to the side and people were setting them up in the space that had earlier been a dance floor.

Peyton made her way over to me. "Hey, you doing okay?"

"Yeah, I'm good. Is it over?" I asked.

"You wish," she said. "No, they're going to go into what we would call a normal youth service. They do different things at this point; we just have to wait and see. So, what do you think of Eric? Isn't he gorgeous?"

"He seems like a nice guy," I said. "What's up with his friends' names—Lamb and Bones? You have to be truly special to have people call you by those names."

She laughed. I could see the soda guy setting up the chairs, too. He moved faster than everyone else and did not chatter like the other guys. When the chairs were almost done, people started taking their seats.

"Ms. Morgan." The voice came from my left as the heavyset woman from the store came out the kitchen.

"Hi, Mrs. Davis," I said cheerily.

She grabbed me and gave me the biggest hug.

"I'm so happy you made it—and you look wonderful," she said.

"Thank you," I said, blushing. That did not stop her.

"I love the new haircut and the curls; they bring out your beautiful complexion and highlight your cheekbones."

"Well, compliments to the stylist," I said as I introduced her to Peyton.

"Oh, I've met Ms. Peyton." Ms. Davis gave her a hug, too. "Well, you girls enjoy yourselves. I'd better resume the service," she said, hurrying to the front of the room.

Peyton and I took seats next to Eric and his friends in the middle of the room. I could see Eric better now; he was quite handsome with a nice smile. Lamb was short and muscular and not much of a looker and Bones was just that–bones.

Ms. Davis went up, greeted the church, and asked all first-time visitors to introduce themselves. One guy got up and introduced himself as Eddie, then Peyton and her friends nudged me to get up.

I got up and said, "I'm Morgan."

"Well, thank you both for coming. I hope you will continue to come each week. I invited Ms. Morgan this week after she played my personal stylist at a great clothing store in town," she added.

I sat down quickly. *She's on a roll tonight*. She introduced her husband, Bishop Davis, who spoke for about thirty minutes about how it was the time for youth to serve the Lord. He was animated on stage, moving about and telling jokes. Everyone laughed aloud.

After that, the service ended. Mrs. Davis announced that there were refreshments in the back. Peyton and I stopped by the kitchen, where the soda guy was helping to serve. I walked up to him ahead of Peyton, who was busy talking to Eric and the others.

He didn't look up, but faced the cooler and asked, "What flavor?

"Grape," I replied.

"Grape?" he repeated, turning to give me a look that said, *Are you serious?* "We don't have grape," he said, expressionless.

"Oh, I'm sorry. Then a coke is fine," I said, flustered.

I could get a good look at him now that he was closer. My stomach dropped. I tried to do everything I could to compose myself before he turned back around. He was flawless! He had smooth dark skin, perfectly formed lips, and piercing eyes. He had a very low haircut with perfect precision at the edges and a thin beard that was just as defined. There was no going back now. My heart started to race and I know that I turned bright red. He turned with a Coke in his hand, his intense eyes narrowing as he handed it to me. He must have seen the change in my appearance.

"Thanks," I managed to say.

I stepped aside to wait for Peyton, still busy conversing with the other three. He got them their sodas, then gave me the slightest look as we walked away. Or so I hoped. I had never had this feeling about a guy before and I was not pleased with myself. *Morgan, get a hold of yourself.*

"Are you okay?" Peyton had run to catch up with me after saying her goodbyes. "You're unusually quiet."

"Oh, I'm fine. It's a lot to take in, but I had a good time."

"Good. So you'll come with me again next Friday," she said happily as she grabbed my arms and skipped to the car.

Chapter 4

September

"You'll be called to see an advisor alphabetically by your last name," said Pam, the registration representative. The weekend was over and there was a week left before school started. The room was filled to capacity with all the incoming freshmen at UWI for Orientation. It had been a long day so far and I thanked God that my last name started with E.

At nine this morning, all the incoming freshmen had lined up with their parents for the tour of the university. Crystal, our tour guide, brought us to the library, the biggest one on the island. Its fancy, beige artistic structure with curves and sharp edges complemented the well-kept campus with large trees shading the students studying on the benches.

"Over here is our courtyard, which we rent to the public for outside events," Crystal said as she cleared the way for us to enter.

We stepped into a breathtaking area, pre-set for a wedding. White wooden chairs were already decorated with flowers; draped fabric connected each row. Palm trees bowed over the structure, giving it perfect shading, just the right amount of light, and a serene atmosphere. Everyone *oohed* and *ahhed* as we walked to the front of the courtyard, but Roxann just stood at the entrance. At the front of the courtyard stood a gazebo completely covered with orchids and orange roses.

I took a deep breath and gazed ahead at the best backdrop ever. A breathtaking view of the mountains spread out behind the gazebo. For just a minute, I felt like I did early in the morning in the country. I met up with Roxann at the entrance. She was smiling.

"Morgan, this is it!"

"This is what?" I asked.

"I didn't know this place existed. This is where I'm going to have my fall fashion show," she said happily.

"Oh, that's nice. I think it would be really pretty," I agreed.

After showing us several buildings where we would have our classes, we visited the cafeteria, the gym, and the dorms. The long tour was tiring, especially since I had already seen most of these places on my tour a few months back, when I first decided to come to UWI.

"Okay everyone, we will now break up in groups!" yelled Crystal, trying to get everyone's attention after the tour. "Parents will join this line and go with Jeffrey to do some real fun activities. You all will be reunited in about an hour for lunch."

Roxann and the other parents left with Jeffrey, a nerdy tour guide who had them march off like they were in boot camp.

"Left! Right! Left! Right!" he yelled as he walked off with a bunch of embarrassing parents, laughing like idiots and shouting right back at him.

Crystal then put us in groups of six for team-building exercises. I had to memorize each person's name, major, and former school for a game called Know Your Circle. Members of the other groups called on random team members to see how well we knew our circles. I was called on once and I answered on point, introducing one of my team members.

"This is Melissa Roberts, her major is psychology, and she attended Queens High," I said boldly.

I wasn't even paying attention when they asked Melissa to introduce me. I just heard, "Morgan Ellis, undecided major, and a former student of Arden High."

I felt so weird when she said undecided. Undecided seemed like it was for losers. After all, the other undecided majors in our group were "sleepyhead Wally" and Ms. "I'm too cool for school." I really wanted to explain that I was different. *I do have some options that I'm weighing. I'm really not a loser.* Instead I just kept quiet, smiled, and dismissed the lousy anxiety that I always felt when discussing this topic.

"I am having a blast!" said Roxann when we joined the other freshmen and parents for lunch. "I would do it all to be in college again. Aren't you excited?"

41

"I would be if I could make up my mind on what I want to do here," I said sadly.

"What do you mean?" she asked. "I thought we decided on business. Remember, you can't go wrong in business."

I said the last part along with her. "I know that's an option, but—"

Crystal shouted, breaking into our conversation. "Can I get everyone's attention please? Say your good-byes, my troopers. We've come to the end of the road for parents and the rest of the day will be devoted to you."

"Oh Morgan, you'll be okay. I'm sure you'll figure it out," my mother said as she squeezed my hand and got up from the table. "I'm going to reserve the courtyard for the fashion show with the event coordinator and I'll see you at home tonight. Okay?"

"Okay. See you," I said, still in my glum mood. When the parents were all gone, we were separated into three rooms to do career testing. I was determined to answer each question as honestly as possible in hopes that the test could make the decision for me.

What are you up to today? I texted Peyton as I waited to see an advisor. They were calling Cs and I knew it would be anytime now that they'll be calling my name. She was probably busy at the salon because she didn't answer.

I looked around the room. It felt like high school all over again. The freshmen all laughed and talked about what they did over the weekend. One girl was telling a group of her friends about a concert that she went to and how she was invited backstage to meet the artists. I even saw some people from my high school, but I didn't talk to them then, so I sure enough wasn't going to talk to them now.

All of a sudden, my mind wandered to my weekend—specifically, to Friday night and the intriguing, name-less guy from church. He had seemed so angry and uptight. *I wonder what his problem is? He was helping out, which should say something about his character, but still he acted distant and unhappy to be there—*

"Morgan Ellis." Pam the registration lady startled me from my daydream.

"Yes, that's me."

I grabbed my bag and went over to her. She took me to a small office in the back.

"Here we are, Morgan. This is your advisor, Ms. Murphy, who will be helping you today with registering for your classes."

I entered the small office and she closed the door.

"Have a seat, Ms. Ellis," said Ms. Murphy. She was quite intimidating with her glasses balanced on her nose, her stern expression, and her unfriendly voice.

"You can call me Morgan," I said, trying to lighten her up.

43

"I call my friends by their first names; you are a student and not my friend, so I will refer to you as Ms. Ellis."

"That's fine, too," I said nervously.

"Now, I see on your file that you are undecided about your major. What exactly are you unsure of?" she asked as she stared at me with her eyes over her glasses.

"Well, I'm thinking about doing…" *Say business first; it will seem like you're more put together.*

"Business," I finally said.

"So, you're not undecided. I'll put you down as a business major then." She began to write on my form.

"No!" I shouted, surprising myself as well.

She stopped abruptly and looked at me.

"Oh, I'm sorry, but I'm thinking about other things, too, like journalism."

"Oh," she said, thoughtfully looking over a long sheet of paper in her hand. Still perusing the paper, she asked, "So why are you considering business?"

I didn't know what to think, but Roxann's silly line popped into my mind. "Because you can't go wrong with business?"

"No, really, why do you think you're interested in this?" she asked, now staring at me.

This woman asked so many questions; I couldn't help thinking that she wanted to give me a hard time.

"Because my mom says so and because she said I may take over her clothing stores one day."

"Is that what you want, Ms. Ellis?"

"I don't know, but maybe if all else fails…"

"Oh, now we are getting somewhere," she said chirpily. "If all else fails. What is the all else?"

There she goes again with the hard, uncomfortable questions. "I don't know what you want me to say. I just don't know what I want to do, that's all." I sounded defensive and annoyed, even to myself.

"Ms. Ellis, one important step in growing up is making decisions, tough decisions! You might not know this, but I'm the advisor assigned to the students who check undecided next to their major. Throughout the years, I've found that ninety percent of the students who say they are undecided actually know exactly what they want to do all along. For some reason, they delay their decision and hold up their lives out of fear and the need to please others. There are classes that you can take as a freshman that can directly affect your course load later in your college career," she said staring at me. "Now, Ms. Ellis, please let me know why you are considering journalism?"

"I guess I want to make a difference," I said nervously. "I mean, I have a passion for telling the story the right way. With the truth, I hope to help those that might not have gotten their stories told otherwise."

She smiled like a proud parent. "Now, was that so hard? I have your results here from the career assessment that you took earlier and I'll give you one guess as to the career that it recommended for you."

I smiled. We both knew what it was.

The streets in Half-Way-Tree were surprisingly calm as I drove home. There were no rallies today, just a few orange-shirt stragglers standing by the bus stop. With the sun about to disappear, the orange sky looked as tired as I felt. I exhaled, surprised at how I felt. I felt almost liberated by the thought that I had made a decision on my career. The knot in my stomach and my normal anxiety about this subject had gone. I glanced at the colorful sky and remembered my prayer. I had prayed for clarity, decisiveness, passion, and happiness. In this one moment, if only for a short time, I embodied all those feelings. Overwhelmed with gratitude, I said a silent prayer and I thanked Him.

My mind suddenly switched to my father, who first introduced me to the idea of journalism. In the second grade, I had been upset because my teacher, Ms. Reid, would beat the students who had the wrong answers to homework questions. It wasn't unusual for teachers to discipline students for misbehaving, but I didn't like the way she beat them for their mental abilities or lack thereof. Although I wasn't the one being beaten with yardsticks and leather belts, I was upset for the students who were. One day after school, I told my father, "I have to find a way to get this to stop."

"Why don't you act like a journalist and write a letter to Ms. Reid with reasons not to beat students for having wrong answers to homework?" he suggested.

"You probably should ask some of the students who get spanked to tell you why they have their homework wrong."

The next day, I went to class early. I had a mission. I interviewed three habitual violators: lazy Eddie, slow David and cry, cry Patrice. I found out that Eddie's mother couldn't read to help him with his homework. We already knew David had learning disabilities so he could not keep up and Patrice had to work nights with her mother, helping her to clean hotels. I wrote a letter to Ms. Reid. Even with my limited vocabulary, I think my passion and my need to help shone through. In my letter I wrote:

Dear Ms. Reid,

I talked to some children in the class. Some Mommys and Daddys cannot read. Some have to work late. And some children don't learn as fast. Please stop beating children when they have the wrong answers on their homework. But try to help by talking to them. Thanks for reading. God bless you.

I had all fourteen students in the class sign it and I brought it to Ms. Reid one morning. She was so impressed that she brought it to the principal and the other teachers. She even took my suggestion. She got David and Eddie signed up for extra lessons and spoke to Patrice's mom, who arranged for Patrice to live with her aunt during the week so she could have some stability.

I was really proud of myself and so was my dad. I remembered sitting at the table after school, telling him about everything that happened. He looked at me with admiration and said, "You will be a great journalist one day."

It was funny that, in this moment of vulnerability, I thought of him. I guess that's how I remembered him—through tears, tears for my mother, my brother, and myself. It was strange to think that, just five years ago, my mother stood in the living room and told us no more tears.

"Have some shame. Don't cry for someone who doesn't cry for you," she had said.

I guess I took it to heart, because I hadn't cried for him since—I didn't think of him much, either.

I pulled up to the house and noticed that there were no cars in the driveway. I checked the mailbox on my way in. With thoughts of my dad flooding my mind, it was ironic that I found an envelope addressed to me. The blue sticker on the top left-hand corner of the envelope had a return address for Sheldon Ellis of Atlanta, Georgia. I held the envelope and flexed it back and forth in my hand, not sure how exactly to feel.

I'd been having a good day. I'd finally allowed myself to let go and enjoy a decision in my life, something he was a part of. This might be the very reason I didn't want to go into journalism. Today, I had confronted my fears and they were already here to haunt me.

I had last heard from my dad three years ago when he had moved to the states with his new pregnant wife, Ivonne. I ran upstairs to put the letter in my room. Then I went back downstairs with a sudden urge to cook dinner.

My phone vibrated in my pocket; Peyton was finally answering my text from earlier today.

What a day, I just got home. No parents here, they must be out schmoozing clients. What you up to?

Nada. Making curry chicken you should come over.

Food, that's all you had to say…see you soon ☺

Peyton's parents owned a real estate company in town, so they often stayed out late, showing properties and attending and hosting open houses. On the weekends, if they had to go out of town, Peyton would visit her big sister Tammy, who lived about four hours away in the city of Montego Bay. During the week, Peyton would just come here if they ran late.

"On the menu tonight, straight from the dutch pot, succulent spicy curry chicken, white rice, sweet plantains and golden corn," I announced as Peyton and I brought the dishes to the table.

Peyton had arrived just fifteen minutes after I invited her over. She had actually helped me with dinner. She made the rice and her famous fruit punch. Roxann and Tony arrived a few minutes after we finished cooking. They were very impressed and surprised. Roxann mostly cooked on Sundays and maybe one other day, but normally we live on takeout.

"Wow, this looks great, girls," Roxann said as she looked at the table covered with all our creations.

"And smells good, too," Tony said as he ran down the stairs to join us at the table. "Who knew you had this in you? Okay, the moment of truth," he said with his fork in hand ready to dig in.

"Wait, we have to pray first," said Roxann.

"That's right—Morgan did cook," Tony joked.

"For your information, I'm a very good cook," I argued.

"Okay, settle down, you two, and close your eyes," Roxann said. "Dear Lord, thank you for the opportunity to be here together as a family. As we are about to eat, I pray that you bless this wonderful meal and bless Morgan and Peyton for preparing it. Help us to always be grateful for all you do and give us more times together like this. Amen."

"Amen," we all said at once.

It was quiet for a little bit. All I could hear were the ting sounds from the forks hitting against the plates as we dished out our food. I think it was a little weird for us all because we didn't do dinner around a table very often, but when Peyton offered to set the table, I didn't stop her.

"This is delicious," Roxann said, breaking the silence.

"Thanks," I said, looking at Tony and sticking out my tongue.

"Well, that's just because Peyton helped you." He looked up at her.

"Actually, I didn't do much—only the rice and drinks. It's all Morgan's handiwork," she said.

"Well, the rice is the perfect texture and the drink is so refreshing," he said winking at her.

She smiled shyly. I just looked at them with a sarcastic look on my face. "Everything is great," Roxann said. "So, what happened at school after I left today?"

"Oh, not much," I said, hoping not to have this conversation. "I did a career assessment, then registered for classes with the advisor."

"So what classes are you taking? What was the result of your assessment?" she pried.

"English Literature, Algebra, Law and Ethics, and Journalism 101."

"I see... so let me guess, the assessment recommended that you go into journalism, right?" she asked in a condescending tone.

"Yes, but I'm just taking two of the classes to see if I'll like it, nothing is set in stone," I said.

Roxann stayed quiet for the remainder of dinner. She had never said why she disapproves of me studying journalism, but I already knew it. It was the same reason that I had reservations about it—journalism was his dream for me. He birthed it in my spirit; he had always said, "My little girl will be the best journalist around one day."

Back then, we had all agreed, but now we wanted it to be a lie just like everything else.

When I got out of the shower, I could hear Peyton and Tony downstairs laughing. After dinner, Peyton offered to do the dishes. I was not at all surprised when Tony, who had never done dishes a day in his life, said he would help. From her sewing room, Roxann's machine whirred away. I found a pair of comfortable shorts and top, then decided to look through some of the books I had bought today for classes. The envelope sat on top of the bag of books.

I had almost forgotten. I really wasn't prepared for this. *Why is he writing me anyway? What can he say now? Do I even care?* All the dormant memories that I thought I had thrown away came back.

Five years ago, he left with the only one explanation. "I have to make myself happy or no one else will."

We later found out that what made him happy was a young woman named Ivonne. He came home one night, sat Roxann down on the couch, and told her that he wasn't happy and that he was leaving.

"Who is she?" Roxann asked. "Don't even lie to me, because I've known for a while now that something is going on."

He paused, then he said, "Her name is Ivonne."

Tony and I sat at the top of the staircase, listening in a state of shock.

"Is this what you really want to do?" Roxann had kept her voice even and calm, but then she broke down, pleading. "Morgan is only thirteen and she adores you. Tony is almost sixteen and needs you in his life, now more than ever. Please don't do this."

"I don't want to lose the kids, but I cannot sacrifice my happiness and sanity for them. I want us to work something out, but leaving Ivonne is not an option," he said sternly.

"Well, you've just made your decision," Roxann said.

He left that night, then came back on the weekend for his stuff. He told me and Tony that he was going away for a while to find himself and to find happiness. He said that he loved us and that we would still see him. After he first left, he sent a few letters and made a few phone calls, then none at all.

With all the heavy emotions surrounding me, I put the envelope back down on my desk and ran downstairs to see what Peyton was up to. As I crossed the living room, I saw her in the kitchen, sweeping.

"Hey, you. You're not done yet?" I asked.

"Almost," she said cheerily.

"Where's Tony?"

"Taking out the garbage," she said.

"Wow, you really have him domesticated!"

He came back in the kitchen as I said that. "So, what do you girls say about a movie?"

"It's late, Tony, and Peyton has to go home," I said, shutting him down.

"Well, I don't have to go home; I could spend the night. Let me just call my mom," she said, stepping into the living room.

Roxann came out of her sewing room with her tape measure around her neck and a pencil behind her ear.

"I'm exhausted," she said. "Tony, please make sure all the doors are locked. Girls, thanks again for dinner. It was really good."

She glanced at me briefly. I smiled, but didn't say anything. I knew she was just trying to be nice since she had shut down after I told her about my journalism class. She had already gotten up the stairs when she called out, "Oh Morgan, I need you to help out at the store all of this week. I have a lot going on. Alright?"

"Yeah, sure. I'll be there."

"Thanks, I owe you," she said, before closing her door for the night.

"Alright, so what are we watching?" Peyton asked.

"Depends on what you guys are in the mood for," Tony said. "I rented *X-Men Wolverine* and *The Fast and the Furious*."

He held out the two movies for us to choose.

"It doesn't matter, both are so *you*," I complained.

"Yeah," Peyton agreed, flopping onto the couch. "Is that really all we have to choose from?"

"Well, Mommy has some others here that she bought last week at MegaMart," Tony said, shuffling through Roxann's collection. "Uh-huh, look what we got here — true chick flicks, *Sense and Sensibility* and *Pride and Prejudice*," he announced.

Peyton and I looked at each other. We had both read most of Jane Austin's books a few years ago and loved them.

"Those are perfect!" Peyton exclaimed.

Tony looked defeated — like he had actually thought Wolverine and some fast cars would stand the test against Mr. Darcy and Mr. Ferrars.

"Alright, calm down," he complained when Peyton and I laughed at him.

"You should have known better than to break those out if you really wanted to watch your movies," I teased.

"You guys are lucky that you cooked or else I wouldn't be this nice," he said.

I felt sure that was not why. If it had been just me and Tony, he wouldn't have been so accommodating.

"Okay, which one?" he asked.

Peyton looked at me. We both smiled and said, "*Sense and Sensibility*."

While Tony put the DVD in, I looked at the clock. It was already 10:45.

"Oh, you guys, I didn't realize it was this late. I have to work at the store tomorrow, so I'll have to do a rain check on the movie," I said, jumping to my feet.

"Oh no, Morgan, but it's *Sense and Sensibility*," Peyton whined.

"I know, but I had a long day and I have an even longer one tomorrow. Don't worry, though. I leave you in good hands—Tony will cry with you," I said, smiling.

"Anthony, do you promise?" Peyton sounded like a lovesick schoolgirl.

"Promise what?" he asked, stepping away from the TV and sitting with Peyton on the couch.

"That you will cry with me," she replied.

He looked at her strangely. I saw the same glimmer that I'd always seen. As I walked up the stairs, I heard him say, "Sure, Peyton, I'll cry with you."

Chapter 5

When I pulled up outside Lee's on Thursday morning, three men in jumpsuits were installing burglar bars around the windows and doors. As I walked in the store, the dust from the construction blew in my direction, getting in my hair, my eyes, and all over my clothes.

"Why don't you just close the store for the week?" I asked Roxann as I walked up to her by the register.

"Oh, don't be silly. It's just a little dust," she snapped back.

"Not to mention the noise," Lisa said, joining us.

Ever since the guy in the orange and green shirt had come into the store last week, my mother has been in an uproar. In Roxann's mind, someone had declared war on her. Since orientation, I'd spent all week at the store, helping her out. Yesterday the guys from Island Securities had worked all day installing an alarm system, along with surveillance cameras inside and outside of the store.

"Look over here, Morgan," Roxann called.

From the far side of the store, she showed me what appeared to be some new clothes on a rack. As I walked over, I noticed that she had two extra racks there.

"What is it?" I asked.

"I took your advice. Here we have two racks devoted to plus-size customers," she said, smiling.

"Oh, that's nice," I said.

All the clothes on the racks had been covered with clear plastic garment bags. I pulled the zipper on one of them, revealing a very stylish and colorful piece.

"I should call Mrs. Davis and let her know that you have some new styles for her."

"That's a great idea," she said. "Tell her to come this afternoon when all the workers are gone. Alright, thanks, my responsible one. I'll see you in three hours," she said.

"Didn't you say you'd be back in two hours?" I asked.

"Oh, yes—I meant two hours," she replied.

I said nothing, even though I know she really meant three or more. Roxann and Lisa left to scout models for her upcoming fashion show. After an hour, the men installing the burglar bars finished for the day and packed up their tools in their big white truck.

"Alright, we're off," said Hector, the man who appeared to be in charge. "Tell Ms. Roxann that we'll be back in the morning to finish up."

"Okay, I'll let her know; see you tomorrow."

He drove off with his workers all piled up in the back of the truck and I finally had some peace and quiet. I swept the floor and wiped off the dust-covered racks. I took out all the clothes that were in garment bags, organizing them evenly on the racks. When I got the store almost back to normal, I sat by the register reading the first chapter of the book for my law and ethics class. I was almost finished when I heard the door chime.

The door to Lee's swung open and a loud, excited voiced filled the room. "Hello there, Ms. Morgan!"

"Mrs. Davis, I didn't even see you coming in," I said, still a bit startled by the door.

"So, what do you have for me today?"

"Well, there are some new pieces over here," I said, directing her to the two racks in the far side of the store.

"Oh, these are really nice. Look at the craftsmanship on this blouse," she said.

"I know; my mom really has a gift for fashion."

"Oh, your mom made these?" she asked, surprised.

"Yes, my mom is the owner and, believe it or not, she designs all of the clothing and makes quite a few of the pieces herself, too."

The door chimed again. I turned to see who it was, but, before I could say anything, Mrs. Davis yelled, "Sean, I'm over here."

It was the guy from church last week. *Oh my God! The guy with the smooth skin, intense eyes but odd demeanor.* I forgot to say something. He walked closer and I noticed that I was standing there like a statue, but nothing came to mind.

"Oh, so you decided to come inside after all," Mrs. Davis said.

"It just occurred to me that I might be waiting for a while," he said.

He had a soothing voice with immaculate diction. His intoxicating cologne complemented his subtle but individual style of dress. He wore dark blue designer jeans with a short-sleeved black shirt with grey designs that fit loosely on his medium built body. His neat black shoes coordinated with his black belt and stylish gray buckle that I couldn't quite see. I could not have put together a better look myself. He didn't say anything as he passed me, but he nodded pleasantly. He went straight to Mrs. Davis and helped her with her handbag, since she had so many clothes in her hands.

"Thanks, my dear," she said to him. "Morgan, you met my nephew Sean last week at church, right?"

"Actually, I don't think I did."

I mean, I saw him—how could I not?—but we didn't officially meet.

"Well, Sean meet Morgan and Morgan, meet my Seanny," she said, rubbing his head.

I smiled as he had embarrassment written all over his face.

"Nice to meet you, Sean," I managed to say.

"Same here," he said with a slight bow and the same pleasant look on his face.

I turned to the racks, pretending to search for something, but actually trying to calm my racing heart.

"These are really nice, Morgan. I'm tempted to take both racks," Ms. Davis joshed.

"Well, that can certainly be arranged," I joked back with her.

Sean walked over to a chair in front of the fitting room and took a seat, which made me happy. I felt a lot more collected and useful with him at a distance.

I coordinated two outfits for Ms. Davis—a long, army green skirt with a fitted tan top that had gold buttons on both sides and a matching belt. The other featured white linen pants with a dark blue top with gray and blue beading around the edges. She picked up some other pieces as I walked her towards the fitting room. Just outside the door, Sean sat with his elbows on his knees and his fingers interlaced, glaring at the floor, deep in thought. For a moment, I wanted to know what he was thinking. He gave me a quick glance as I passed by. I stayed focused, hanging his aunt's clothes in one of the rooms.

"Here we are," I said, stepping out and closing the door behind me. "Just let me know if you need help with anything."

Of course, he was still sitting there. This time, he gave me a shy half-smile, then looked away. I walked straight to the register, determined not to appear fazed by his presence. I tried to finish reading the first chapter in my law and ethics book, but to no avail. I was reading, but not concentrating. *Why does this nobody have this effect on me?*

I managed to glance over where he was sitting. Now he was staring at his phone screen and moving his hands, probably either playing a game or texting someone. *Of course, he is texting someone—a girl, I'm sure*. I tried to look away, but, for some reason, he mesmerized me. Yes, he was gorgeous, but I'd seen gorgeous guys before, some of them interested, gorgeous guys. I hadn't given them a chance or a second look.

The door to the fitting room shuffled; Mrs. Davis appeared in the green skirt and tan top that I picked out for her.

"So, what do you think?" she asked Sean with her hands on her waist.

I took that as a good sign, since Roxann always said that a woman feels confident and attractive when she poses with her hand on her waist. I closed my book and walked over to the fitting room. I could hear Sean telling her she looked very nice.

"Well, Ms. Morgan picked out this outfit," she said to him as I approached.

"Oh, you are styling," I said.

"Do you really like it?" she asked with her hands on her waist again.

She did look younger and I could tell that she really liked the outfit, so I made the sale with the compliments. "The skirt is the perfect length, hitting just below your knees. It's not too fitted, so you can be comfortable yet fashionable. The buttons on the top add character and the belt accentuates your figure perfectly."

By the time I finished, she was twirling and pivoting like she was walking on an actual runway. We all laughed at this, including Sean, who seemed amused by his aunt's antics. She ran back into the fitting room to try on the other outfit.

"Don't move, Morgan; I'll be out in just a minute," she shouted.

My smile vanished. Left to stand in front of this nerve-racking, intimidating guy, I twitched my fingers, trying to look anywhere but towards him. The heavy beating of my heart moved into my throat; I couldn't have talk even if I had wanted to. The silence was deafening. The elephant in the room was stifling me. As I stood there uncomfortably, Sean seemed to be in another world. He even chuckled to himself. I don't know what got into me, but I took his private chuckle as an icebreaker and I actually spoke.

"Your aunt is really funny," I said.

He shook his head, but said nothing. I wished I had just kept my mouth shut; obviously he did not want to make conversation. I moved towards the plus-size rack, once again pretending to fix clothes. I glanced over. He sat in the same position, bent over, fingers linked, deep in thought, and, seemingly, doing just fine.

Soon after, to my relief, Mrs. Davis stepped out of the fitting room more invigorated than before. She emerged slowly, making a grand entrance. The pants draped nicely and the intricate beading on the blouse dressed up her outfit. She held her shoulders back; I could tell her spirits were high. In fact, her whole posture had changed since she had slouched into the store wearing a big jean skirt with a plain white t-shirt.

Now her whole face lit up; she looked younger and more stylish.

"Really nice, Aunty. You should get both outfits," said Sean.

He sounded less than enthused, yet as if he wanted to say more. I smiled at Mrs. Davis. She knew she looked beautiful and I didn't have to say a word.

Sean

The summer after court

The juniper trees hung low, drooping in the early morning dew and, like the sun, not ready to wake. In the crisp, clean air, only the burble of the lazy river water could be heard whirring in the distance.

Sean moved the dried-up flowers and replaced them with her favorites— blue hydrangeas and yellow tulips. As if he did not want to wake her, he spoke softly.

"I'm sure you already know that I'll have to leave for a little while. I miss you. Don't know why I'm saying goodbye, when you're with me all the time... Ms. Nelly will bring fresh flowers each week and she'll bring Junie down from time to time. And I'll be back; I just need to put this behind me. I love you."

A few hours later, he finally pulled up to the address. The sign outside the house read, "Jamaica Housing Trust Building Project." He parked behind a dirty blue truck, overflowing with old tools. He heard the huffs of loud trucks in the distance, the beeping sound as they backed up, tools hammering and voices shouting in the distance. A few cars lined one side of street. He peered down the row of houses, noticing other unfinished ones. The other side of the road was void of homes and life. Based on the cement trucks and lingering white dust, the huge yellow aluminum structure appeared to be a cement factory.

He pushed the gate of the house open and recognized his aunt right away as the no-nonsense, heavyset woman in a long denim skirt and sneakers, arguing.

"I can work out here, too, not because I'm a woman nuh mean I have to be inside the house."

"Fine, suit yourself. If you want to stay out in the blazing sun, it's up to you," his uncle said to her. His slender body slouching as he disappeared around the side of the house.

Sean's aunt picked up a big fork tool and started digging. He passed some men putting wooden post in the ground on his way over to her. Pushing hard, she removed the visor to wipe the sweat from her forehead and spotted him right behind her.

"Oh Seanny, you made it!" She pulled off the thick gray gloves and hugged him tightly. "How was the drive in?"

"You know me–nothing to it," he said, hugging her back. "So, I see you're hard at work."

"Yes, my love, look what they have me out here doing," she said with a smirk on her face. "But it's all for a good cause; these families need these homes and we're finally on the home stretch. They're already putting in the post for the fence."

"See? Right there." She pointed to the men at the side, then put her foot on the fork. "I'm digging holes about two feet deep, so they can run the pipes around the house. The women are busy inside, painting and cleaning all the dust away, you know."

"So what you doing out here, Aunty?" Sean asked.

She slapped him with the gloves. "I'm as good as any of these men. I don't have to be stuck inside cleaning bathrooms; I do that enough at home."

They laughed.

She handed him one of the tools and told him to start digging around the side. He looked down at his shoes, already white with dust. He sighed. He saw some rain boots on the porch of the house and left his shoes beside them, rolled up his pants, and put the boots on. He took his shirt off, leaving only his gold chain and watch. As he walked down the steps toward his post, the chatter inside the house stopped. He spun around to find all the women staring in silence. He paused, then continued. As he turned the corner, he heard a loud cackle.

That evening, his aunty had her legs on his uncle and an ice pack on her head, while Sean brought her some water. "Thank you, love," she said with exhaustion on her face. "I didn't get to make up your bed yet, but the sheets are folded on the chair in the room."

"Don't worry, Aunty. I got it," Sean said. She had given them quite a scare earlier. One minute, she had been digging and the next, some of the guys had run behind the house, yelling for his uncle to come quick. Sean had run back with them, only to see his aunt passed out on the grass.

"Heat exhaustion," the paramedics had said as they strapped her to the stretcher and treated her in the ambulance. They all had been concerned, but, after everyone found out that she was okay, several people turned away to hide their grins. Everyone knew how headstrong she could be.

Sean walked through the neat and tidy house toward his room. His aunt and uncle had never had children, so everything stayed organized and in its place. At the end of the passage, the room at the back of the house was dark, but the light from outside came through the windows, making the shadows of the nearby tree dance on the wall. He dropped his bags on the floor and stood there for a while, looking into the darkness. Everything was quiet. Before moving from the door, he wondered how he'd gotten to this place of uncertainty and unresolved questions, with no one to count on and no one he could trust.

He moved to the bed, propping the pillow up. He didn't want to be angry, but that's all he had in him. Just last year, he had been getting better, trying to move past the mishaps of life. And the moment that he put himself out there, he got burnt. At that point, he had decided that he would never let his guard down again. Now, on his first night in Kingston, he decided he would stay focused and just do his time. He had no time for fun and games.

"Just do what you have to do and put it behind you," his mom would say. Of course, back then, she had meant trivial things like doing his homework and taking out the trash.

Some would say that he had been lucky to get a job at *Urban News*, the sister company of the company he worked for in Port Antonio. And that he had been lucky that his father convinced the courts to assign him community service at his aunt's church, so he could stay in her home. Yet, lucky or blessed, he still had too much anger to even see the good in that. He would try to be cordial to his aunt and uncle until he could move on with his life, but that was all.

Roxann pressed down hard on the horn.

"Get the hell out the way and go get a job!" she yelled.

The group of JLP supporters dancing in the street had traffic backed up about seven blocks. Yesterday on the news, Rachel Lawson had reported that there would be a JLP rally late Friday afternoon. No one had

imagined that the supporters would be out in numbers
this early in the morning.

With all the craziness predicted in the streets today,
Roxann had closed Lee's for the day. She still had to
familiarize herself with all the new gadgets that she
had installed. Then, for some reason, she had thought
she could go across town to Aunty Madge's office and
get back home before the crowds gathered. That left
us weaving in and out of traffic on a road filled with
cars and crazy people. Roxann accelerated, going right
for a group of guys who refused to move out the way.
She slammed on the brakes just before hitting a guy
who was busy twirling in the air on the back wheel of
his bicycle. Frightened, the guy quickly slammed his
bicycle back on the ground. He and the other loiterers
threw their hands up at us and started to cuss.

I had not seen Roxann so angry in a long time. She
stuck her head out the window and screamed, "The next
time, I won't miss. I swear!"

"Mommy, put your head back inside!" I said
frantically.

The drivers around us blew their horns, the noise
deafening. Scared out of my mind, I asked, "Where are
all the police?"

"Sure, the police—they're all a part of this corruption and indecency, too. You think they care?" Roxann
screamed.

I just slid down in my seat and kept quiet. Clearly,
this was too much for me. I could still hear the horns

of the cars around us bellowing and Roxann joined in with force. The people continued cussing, even as they cleared the street. Before they were completely gone, Roxann hit the gas pedal, passing them so fast that they jumped out of the road onto the sidewalk. Roxann was the definition of road rage, coupled with the indignant demonstrators, made a lethal combination.

I didn't like when she got so angry. Sure, the men had no business gallivanting in the street, but the way the anger consumed her could not be healthy. In the complete silence, Roxann's face still wrinkled with disgust as she sped through the town.

"Mom, you really have to take it easy," I began to say.

"Take it easy, huh? While people who are going nowhere waste my time? I should have run them over and teach them to stay on the sidewalk or, better yet, in their shacks," she said, still angry.

I didn't bother saying anything else. Obviously she felt how she felt. Nothing I said would make a difference.

We pulled up to Aunty Madge's office about twenty minutes later. Roxann's wild imagination had led to this whole meeting. She bumped into Aunty Madge last week while food shopping and babbled about her upcoming fashion show and how she wanted this year's show to be real special.

Aunty Madge mentioned that her company was building new structures all over town and needed to do some advertising. She and Peyton had been dropping off flyers at the front of the store when Roxann spotted them.

"If you don't mind, Roxann, can you leave a stack of these at Lee's?" Aunty Madge asked. "I know that you have some real well-off customers who might just be interested."

Roxann's eyes opened wide. She bit her lips as if to prevent herself from exploding.

"What is it?" Aunty Madge asked her.

And that conversation got Roxann's wild imagination going. She had to have Aunty Madge's building models as the backdrop of her show.

Walking into the meeting, we saw that Aunty Madge's office had been made into a showroom. She had three miniature models set up in the office.

"Oh my! Morgan, aren't these lovely?" Roxann immediately ran over to the tallest building adorned with small, boxed windows illuminated with lights. "This one is ideal for my uptown scene."

It really was spectacular. "Look at the little cars!" I said excitedly.

"Oh my, isn't that something? This is more than I had imagined." She stood there in amazement, staring at the brightly lit skyscraper decked out with a sparkling mirrored surface. In front of the mini palace, little cars, bumper to bumper like rush hour in Half-Way-Tree, filled a long, winding road. I have to say it was a true work of art.

"The show will be nothing short of perfect. Look at this—they look so real," Roxann carried on.

Just then, Aunty Madge came out of the back in a long, green summer dress with a camera in hand.

"Good morning, ladies!" She smiled, greeting us with her loud, vibrant voice. She looked at Roxann. "I can see you like the models."

"What's not to like? When I told you I wanted your buildings as a backdrop for the show, I thought you had a canvas drawing of some sort, not actual buildings," Roxann explained.

"Well, it so happened that, after I spoke to you, I went to an art show in New Kingston. I met this talented young man who had these models for sale. He told me he makes these exquisite buildings as a hobby. I got a really good price on these three and I was thinking that he might even be willing to rent us some more to use at the show—Oh Morgan, Peyton is in the office in the back, fast asleep," Aunty Madge said with a grin.

"That sounds just like her," I said as I walked past the other models to the office.

The last model caught my eye; it represented a quiet, old fashioned coffee shop. I fell in love; it had its own unique character and charm. It even smelled like coffee. It had big, low to the ground windows, with detailed trim and little fake people sitting around small tables and chairs with mugs in hand. A white picket fence and trees surrounded it, like a coffee shop in the country. I could see myself sitting there in a long, fluffy dress and old-fashioned hairdo like the women from *Sense and Sensibility*. As I pushed the door to Aunty Madge's office, I thought how great it must feel to be an artist. I would love to be able to bring out the beauty in something so ordinary.

I found Peyton fast asleep on the couch in Aunty Madge's office. "Wake up, sleepyhead."

"What is it?" She frowned as she turned slowly around to face me. "Oh, it's you. I am so tired," she said, turning her back to me, then adding, "And hungry."

"Alright, let's go," I said.

"Go where?"

"To get some food."

"Don't you see the road is a mess with the election rally and all?" she said.

"How could I forget? Mommy almost ran over some of the people in the street this morning. She is crazy!" I said.

Peyton, who found everything funny, laughed aloud, jumped to her feet, and said, "Alright, let's go."

"I thought you said—" She was already through the door. I mumbled, "Never mind."

Peyton opened the back door quietly, signaling for me to hurry up before our moms realize we were gone. I could hear Roxann telling Aunty Madge about her excitement with the loiterers this morning. By the time I got outside in the heat and hustle and bustle of vehicles on the road, Peyton had gotten far ahead.

"Where are we going?" I yelled over the noise.

"To get coffee," she yelled back.

I ran a little and finally caught up to her. She tilted her head back, inhaling the polluted air. "Freedom!"

"You know they're going to kill us, right?" I said.

"Yeah, but we won't be long. Besides, parents live for things like this," she said nonchalantly.

"Things like what?" I asked.

"Children being defiant and not doing what they are always supposed to do," she replied. "Just imagine if you always listened to them, then they wouldn't have a purpose. Think about it!" she said, convinced of her notion.

"Sure, Peyton. I guess that's your theory and you're sticking to it.

"Yup," she said.

In the vicious heat from the sun, I wished more than ever that I was not wearing jeans and a long-sleeved top. I should have dressed more like Peyton in her short, cotton, breezy dress. She skipped ahead, spinning around like a little girl. That was so like Peyton to find the fun in any situation, even if we were walking on the street at a dangerous time when sensible people were staying home.

The light turned red at the intersection and we ran across the street to Nora's Café.

"See that wasn't so bad," smirked Peyton.

"Not yet, at least," I snapped back.

The café was quiet as we walked in. The smell of the Blue Mountain Peak coffee was strong in the air. A huge showcase of tantalizing pastries lined the front of the store.

"Hey, there. What can I get you ladies today?" asked the short man who emerged from the back room wearing a floury apron.

"Everything looks so yummy," I said.

"I think I want one of everything," Peyton remarked. "Let's start with one small coffee and a hot chocolate for my friend here — better yet, make that three small coffees. I have a feeling we will need to do some buttering up," she said, laughing.

"Good call," I agreed.

"And a slice of the banana bread and the carrot cake," she added.

The frosting on the marble cake called my name. "And I'll have a slice of your marble cake, please."

"Coming right up," he said, smiling.

Behind me, Peyton sat at a table looking out at big, busy Kingston Street.

"Oh, look over there, Morgan." She pointed towards several police cars blocking the street while three police officers in neon vests unpacked cones and barricades. They were obviously preparing for the rally this Afternoon.

"You can pick up your orders over here." The short man signaled for me to meet him at the register, interrupting my thoughts.

After I picked up our items, Peyton still sat comfortably where I left her.

"Are we going?" I asked.

"Let's eat first," she complained.

"Peyton, don't you see that they are already getting started outside? Anty Madge and my mother will be wondering where we are any moment now," I said, suddenly regretting my decision to come out.

"I'm starving and the rally won't start for hours," she whined.

"Okay, okay—but we have to hurry up." I gave in and sat down.

"Now, was that so hard?" she smiled. She opened her bag, took a bite of her carrot cake, and looked like she was in heaven.

"That good, huh?" I asked.

"Too good, too good," she said, smiling.

We sat there eating and she closed her eyes making funny expressions with every bite.

We laughed.

"So, in two days you'll be a college student. Excited?" she asked in between bites.

"I guess so. I'd be more excited if I was going abroad for school or something," I said.

"Is that what you want—to go abroad?"

"Not really. I'm just saying that going to UWI will be like going to high school all over again, but without you."

"Your dad lives in Georgia, right?"

"I think so, why?"

"Well have you thought about going to school there? I mean, it's somewhere different and new. It would be exciting and you could meet his new family," she said.

I knew she probably just meant to tease me, but I couldn't help answering sarcastically. "I don't want to go abroad that bad. I'm fine with UWI. I'm just cranky today—it's early," I said.

"I'm sure it will be great. And you know what's better?" she asked.

"What?" I asked.

"Where we are going later," she said with her childish excitement.

I pretended not to know what she meant, just to mess with her. Mrs. Davis reminded me about youth meeting yesterday, when she and her nephew were in Lee's.

"What day is it?" I asked.

"Friday," she said, looking at me suspiciously. Her tone got stern. "You are coming with me tonight, Morgan."

"Of course I'm coming with you. After all, this might be the last Friday night. Next week I'm a college student and I might not have time for little church groups."

"Yeah, yeah," she said.

"You only want to go and see that redbone anyway."

"That is not true," she argued. "I go to praise God. Networking and making friends is not a bad thing, either. You should try it. I can't be your only friend forever."

"Hardly," I said, getting up from the table. "I have lots of friends."

"Anthony doesn't count," she teased.

As we walked outside into all the noise, I barely heard her say, "maybe you should invite him tonight."

Outside, we held hands to cross the street. I could feel something brewing in the air. The man in the taxi next to us started arguing with another taxi driver. A group of police blocked off the street, blowing their whistles loudly. The chaos before the rally had already started. This was no place for two timid girls.

"We better hurry and get back to the office," Peyton said.

We walked briskly, Peyton clutching my left hand while I balanced the coffees in my right.

"Nice lady, come give me a talk nuh, is that for me?" a dirty old man asked, touching my arm as I passed by.

I quickly moved my arm away, spilling a little coffee on my shirt. "Great."

"Don't worry; it will come out. Just keep walking," Peyton said.

Up ahead on the sidewalk, some men in orange huddled, clearly wanting to start trouble at the JLP rally.

They screamed at some people in green across the road. As we approached them, profanity ran rampant.

Peyton walked close to the road and muttered under her breath, "Don't make any eye contact."

I faced straight ahead and, despite their yelling, pretended they weren't even there. I could see Aunty Madge's office now.

"You can look, you know," one guy in a green bandana yelled. "We won't bite."

We kept walking, holding tight to each other's hands. Frightened and nervous, we quickly turned the knob to the back door of Aunty Madge's office. We were about to take a big sigh of relief, but held it as we saw both our moms' angry faces staring at us.

"Coffee?" I asked, even though I knew I looked like I'd just seen a ghost.

"Morgan Lee Ellis, you're playing with your life, you know," Roxann said in a heated tone. "It is a dangerous world out there and you need to take heed."

"You girls have to be more careful," Aunty Madge continued in a more subdued manner. "This is not the time for young girls—or anyone, for that matter—to be roaming the streets. Innocent people are dying every day during this election period, just because they're in the wrong place at the wrong time."

"We're so sorry," Peyton said.

"Yes, you both are right. We should have known better," I said.

"I know I'm right," Roxann said.

As she walked away swiftly, she shouted, "This no country for young fools!"

Aunty Madge gave us her disappointed look and followed suit. Peyton and I closed the door to her mom's office.

For a minute, we both shared a look of remorse and fright, especially after the scary encounter outside. Then Peyton burst out in uncontrollable laughter.

"What?" I asked, not sure if I missed the joke.

"That was freaking crazy," she managed to say. "I need to stop hanging around you, Morgan."

"Hanging out with me?" I complained.

"You almost got us killed by a mob and our moms. You're a bad influence on me!" We both started to laugh.

"I really was frightened by those men, Peyton," I said, almost in tears.

"And Anty Roxann frightened me," Peyton said, laughing. She mimicked Roxann perfectly, "Morgan Lee Ellis, you are playing with your life. This is no country for young fools!"

Our laughter quickly stopped when we heard Roxann's voice, "Where is Morgan with those coffees?"

After a moment of silence, we burst out laughing again.

Chapter 6

I pulled up to Oasis at 8:20 that night, spotting Peyton's car close to the front of the building. She had gone ahead of me since Roxann had me on the road all day, getting things prepared for her fashion show. After we had left Peyton and her mom earlier, we had visited the fashion studio that was sewing Roxann's designs. I even had to play mannequin and do some test walks so they could alter some clothes.

"Morgan, you really should think about being a model in the show," Roxann said.

"I don't know, we'll see," I said.

We visited the party planner to finalize scenes and décor. Exhausted and late for church, I barely had time to run home and change. I decided on a long gray dress with a green necklace and matching sandals to help pull off a quick, thoughtless look.

The parking lot was full and quiet. I could barely hear any sound coming from the church. I started to leave, but something prodded me to stay. After all, I was starting school on Monday and I wanted to start off on the right foot. I had already accepted that everything in my life was unsure and I needed God's guidance more than ever. I decided to say a little prayer before I went in.

God, help me to push beyond my feelings. I pray that you allow something magical and special to happen in your service tonight so I can know that you are still there. Amen.

I went into the entryway of the church, where the silence persisted. This was nothing like last week. There was no sign of a nightclub, but, then again, I was also an hour late. I got up on my toes and peeped through the glass into the church. Everyone was in pairs, doing an exercise, talking and engaged. I saw Peyton standing in front of redbone Eric, animated and laughing. I smiled as I saw her. I could only imagine what she was saying to the boy.

Not sure if I wanted to go in by myself, I reached for my phone to call her. The next thing I knew, the door swung open. My phone, keys, and right sandal flew in all directions. I ended up flat on the ground, disoriented from the blow and with a burning sensation building in my nose. I heard running feet, then someone stood over me.

"Oh my God, are you okay?" he asked. I tried to get up, but he said, "Don't move. I'll help you up."

I managed to look up at him scrambling with his clothes. He took off his black polo shirt, leaving only his white undershirt. He bent down to give me the black shirt, then stopped. "This is too rough."

He jumped back to his feet, taking off his white t-shirt instead. *I must be in a dream.* Even in my frazzled state, I noticed his perfect body that matched his perfect face. In no time, he knelt by my side again, this time with his white t-shirt and bare body. He handed me the shirt. "Keep this on your nose; it will help with the bleeding."

"Bleeding?" I asked as I tried to get up again.

"Let me help you," he said again. "Take your time. I need to get you on a chair in the kitchen, so you can keep your head back. Do you think you can walk?"

"I think so," I said in the most unconvincing way I knew how.

"That's alright. Would it be okay if I carried you?" he asked.

How cute, I thought. *He asked me if he could carry me.*

I decided not to be a weakling. With his help, I made it to the kitchen. The throbbing in my nose grew even stronger, so I squeezed the shirt tightly against it and sat down. I could smell his cologne in the shirt and I kept it pressed against my nose a little longer. He tilted my head back on the chair and told me to close my eyes. I heard the freezer open, then he was back with an icepack.

"Can I see?" he asked, gently tugging his t-shirt away from my nose. "Ohh," he said. His face looked like he was in pain. "Morgan, I'm so sorry."

He remembers my name. I lit up inside. "Is it that bad?"

He smiled. "No, it is just a bit swollen. I meant I'm sorry for knocking you over."

"Don't worry about it," I said, sounding nasal and still in extreme pain. "It was an accident—plus, I should have been paying attention."

"No, it was me," he said. "I was carrying sodas to the kitchen and used my back to push the door open."

"The pain will be over tomorrow," I said with my head still hung back over the chair.

Sean didn't say anything else, but he stared at me with deep apologetic eyes. "I know!" he said, jumping to his feet.

"You know what?" I asked, my voice sounded muffled under his shirt on my nose.

I followed him with my eyes as he went to the refrigerator and took something out. He kept it hidden, looking even more spectacular when he returned with a grin on his face. I didn't think I had ever seen him smile before. He ceremoniously revealed a can of grape soda balanced on one hand. Almost bowing, he said, "For you, madame."

With my heart pounding, I moved my body into an upright position and took the soda.

"Thank you," I said, clearing my throat and feeling a bit vulnerable and flushed. I knew it was just a soda, but, for some reason I couldn't help feeling that he had brought it especially for me. *Would he ever have gotten this flavor if I hadn't asked for it last week?* I was confused. *He was actually thinking of me. How weird is that? I'm reading into something that may be nothing.* I looked up at him and, when our eyes met, I quickly turned away. Obviously, he found my discomfort funny. I heard quiet laughter.

The door swung open. Everyone rushed into the kitchen for refreshments. The full room and the loud chatter made it impossible to hear what Sean was saying. I guess he said I should move because he helped me up and brought me to a bench in an isolated corner next to the water fountain.

"You should be safe right here. I don't want anyone else running you over." He smiled. "Will you be okay? I'm going to serve them and I'll be right back!" he shouted.

"I'll be fine!" I shouted back.

He jumped over the counter and began serving. I looked through the crowd. Peyton was talking to Eric and his friends. I stood up and waved, trying to get her attention, but she was wrapped up in her conversation. I sat back down and text her.

I'm here, sitting by the water fountain.

Of course, she didn't hear the beep on her phone and continued talking.

Sean worked fast, not interacting with anyone. He just did the task at hand. Now and then he looked over at me. I glanced at him from the corner of my eye, but I avoided making eye contact. *Bad combination!* As the room cleared, Peyton moved toward the front of the line. I heard her telling her friends that I was supposed to have come tonight. Then she looked at her phone and turned around, confused. She walked towards me, looking surprise to see me hidden in the corner. *The corner where Sean tucked me away!*

"Morgan, when did you get here? Why didn't you come get me?"

Before I could answer, she said, "Are you okay? You look different."

I showed her the bloody shirt in my hand and, before I could explain, she went into Peyton mode.

"Oh my God, what happened? Where are you bleeding?"

"I got hit in the nose — by accident," I added quickly.

The room had almost cleared, so I knew that Sean could hear me, even though he didn't look our way.

"Oh honey, I'm sorry," she said, concerned.

"I'm okay. It's not hurting that much anymore," I said.

She stared at my face. "Oh, I can see it now. It's just a bit swollen; it should go down in time for school on Monday. So, what happened?"

Before I could answer, Eric and his friends all came closer, also wanting to know how my accident happened.

"Well—" I started, then Sean stepped in.

"I'm the culprit," he said, looking at Peyton. "I wasn't looking and I knocked her over with the door."

He turned to me with his sincere, apologetic eyes and I looked away quickly.

"Oh," said Peyton, looking at us hesitantly and suspiciously. "Well, I'm sure she'll be fine."

"Yeah, I'm fine," I said to him.

I smiled, not giving in to the weak feeling that I had from his obvious impact on me. I stared into his eyes confidently, without flinching or looking away. I think this surprised him—I mean, it surprised me!

"Okay, then. I hope you feel better in the morning and, again, I'm really sorry," he said, stepping away so we could get by.

"No hard feelings," I said, trying to smile as I walked off toward the parking lot with Peyton and her crew.

I sat in my car while Peyton said her goodbyes, hoping she hadn't heard the heavy beating of my heart. I was relieved when she waved to me and got into her car. Needless to say, my relief was short-lived as she pulled up behind me in the driveway to my house.

"Alright missy," she said as she closed her car door.

Before I opened my own car door, I took a deep breath, preparing to face her accusations.

"Hey, I didn't know you were planning on stopping." I fumbled in my bag for my keys while trying to act as natural as possible.

"And leave my best friend by herself while she's in pain? Never!"

"Oh, it's not that bad really. The pain went away a while ago," I lied.

"I'm sure! I got a really good look at your medication," she said. "Intense, I tell you."

"What in God's name are you talking about, Peyton?"

"Nothing. Don't mind me," she said with a grin on her face.

My nose felt a little heavy and numb and I dreaded my first look in the mirror. I opened the door, happy to see Tony rushing down the stairs, dressed in nice jeans and a long-sleeved striped shirt.

"Hey, you two. You guys are home early."

"It's not early, Tony, it's almost ten," I said.

"My point exactly—and it's Friday night. Even Mommy has gone out tonight and she just left."

"He does have a point, Morgan," Peyton said.

"Well, I don't care; I was at church," I said to Tony.

"Well, hardly, Morgan; I was a church," Peyton pointed out. "You were busy playing doctor and patient with Mr. Soda Man," she laughed.

"Oh, shut up! I was not!"

"What happened now?" Tony asked, fighting to roll up his sleeves.

"Nothing," I said, skipping the details. "I bumped into someone and barely hit my nose."

"Barely, huh? I knew something looked different. Your nose is huge!" he said, laughing.

"It is not," Peyton said, giggling, obviously amused by Tony.

I walked over the mirror, almost in panic, to look at the fate of my nose. It felt worse than it looked. Actually, it didn't look bad at all.

"Shut up, Tony," I fussed.

He didn't answer, probably because Peyton was helping him to roll up his sleeves. He looked at her while she did it. He stared at her hair, at her face, at her. *How weird*. It was almost like I wasn't in the room.

"So where are you off to tonight?" I asked Tony as I clicked on the TV.

"Movies," he said.

"Oh, what are you seeing?" Peyton asked.

"Mi nuh know, so much to choose from."

Feeling a little mischievous, I asked the obvious question. "And who's the unlucky girl?"

Peyton looked up at him and Tony looked away.

"Who said anything about a girl?" he asked.

"Oh sure, you're going to the movies by yourself or with a bunch of your guy friends," I said sarcastically.

"Actually, I didn't invite anyone yet. If you must know, I was going to call my friend Sarah who is visiting from New York to see if she wanted to go," he said, trying to sound casual.

"Friend, huh?"

"Yes, just friends," he said, glancing at Peyton even though I asked the question.

I think I'm enjoying this a little too much.

"But you two are welcome to come if you want to," he said.

"And cramp your style?" I said. "We'll pass."

"I mean, I wouldn't bother calling Sarah if you guys want to come," he clarified.

"Why not?" Peyton asked. "It shouldn't matter if she's just your friend."

I chuckled as I watched Tony try to talk himself out of the tangled web he'd woven. I walked into the kitchen to get an ice pack for my aching nose. When I returned, Peyton informed me that we were going to the movies with Tony. She said that there was this movie that she really wanted to see, even though she couldn't remember its name at the moment. I could tell that she was inviting me out of courtesy.

"Peyton, I have a damn near broken nose. I'm going to get some rest. You guys go on and have fun."

"Are you sure?" Tony asked.

"I'm sure," I said.

And, just like that Peyton and Tony, left on their first date. I chuckled at their transparency as they walked towards his car. He opened and closed the door for her. He even looked nervous.

As I walked up the stairs to bed, I couldn't help thinking about Sean. I had seen a new side of him tonight. *That, I can get used to.* He had been charming and caring and smiled a lot. *Who knew?* He had been engaging and he had brought me a grape soda.

The cold icepack numbed my throbbing nose. I left it there as I lay in bed, staring up at the ceiling. I started drifting off to sleep, but my imagination constantly interrupted.

I wanted to know him more. He felt like the missing piece of the puzzle, the one who would help my life make sense. I had no assurance that I'd be pleased if I knew more, yet I still felt an almost unnatural need for him.

In my prayer that night, I prayed for relationships, a prayer I don't think I've ever prayed before. I prayed for the relationship between my mom and me to be stronger, for the relationship between my dad and all of us to be fixed. I prayed for Peyton and Tony, for any semblance of a relationship they had to be realized. And last but not least, I prayed for Sean. I mean, I really prayed for Sean.

Grandma Lilith always said, "Be careful what you pray for; you just might get it."

I woke up early Saturday morning when Roxann called me from the bottom of the stairs.

"I'm still sleeping!" I yelled back.

"Morgan, you have a visitor," she said.

I heard her tell someone that I normally sleep in on Saturdays. With my eyes burning and my nose tender, my entire face ached. I stretched for my phone to see the time. To my surprise, the display lit up, showing 8:47. *Who comes to someone's house at this ungodly hour in the morning?*

I smelled what I presumed to be Roxann's specialty—*ackee* and saltfish and roast breadfruit, so I figured it must be Peyton. She probably fell asleep on the couch after her late-night rendezvous with Tony. *But she would have come upstairs*. With the sun shining through my window, I could not possibly fall back asleep. Convinced that Roxann was making some manipulative attempt to wake me up to help her, I rolled out of bed and walked down the stairs with my hair a mess and in my old nightgown. Slouching, I yawned to prove a point before I said, "Hey, Mom, what is it?"

"Hey, you. Look who's here," she said cheerily. "Your friend from church."

If I could have run and crawled in a hole, I would have. I have never looked so busted before. I had not worn this nightgown in years; it was short, tight, and faded. Roxann had made matching ones for me and Peyton when we were twelve. I never wear it, but Peyton saved hers and convinced me to do the same. I stored it in the drawer at the bottom of my bed with some other old stuff. Last night, I had felt lazy and didn't want to get back up, so I reached in that drawer

92

and this came out. *Oh my God, I'm caught in rags with unwrapped, unruly hair! Scream!*

"Oh, hi," I said. I know I had a confused look on my face. "What are you…?"

I couldn't think straight since the only thing in my head was *Abort, abort!*

"Would you excuse me a minute? I'll be right back," I said as I quickly spun around. Once out of sight, I did a mad dash up the stairs to my room. I closed the door behind me and wondered if I was dreaming.

"Oh my God," I kept saying, over and over again. I dropped face down into the pillow and screamed. "Ouch!" I had forgoten about my nose.

"Okay, Morgan, you have to get a hold of yourself," I said quietly.

I wasn't sure if I was mad at Roxann for calling me downstairs without a heads up or confused about why Sean was in my house. *Definitely Roxann!*

But, for now, that didn't matter. I had to get myself looking like someone. I jumped in and out the shower in less than three minutes. I grabbed the first thing I could find in the dress section of my closet, a turquoise summer dress. I pulled it over my head, brushed my teeth, and pulled my hair back in a ponytail, then got back down the stairs in less than seven minutes.

Sean sat at the table eating with Roxann, deep in conversation about Roxann's upcoming fashion show.

She was telling him about how difficult it has been to bring everything all together.

"There is always something more to do; it's much more than finding the place, clothes and models, it's the little things I tell you. I think I'm done and then here comes the music, lighting, marketing, and not to mention planning the details to create the right ambiance...," she said, as he looked at her, listening and nodding.

When I walked towards them, they stopped the conversation to look in my direction. Sean stared at me and my knees lost function. I held on to one of the chairs at the table for support.

"Don't you clean up nicely?" Roxann said.

I ignored her comment to give her a glaring stare that said, *I can't believe how you let me come down earlier.*

She obviously got my point, because she said, "Oh, sweetie, you know you are gorgeous."

Embarrassed, yet curious, I glanced at Sean. He smiled, but looked away, probably to spare me additional humiliation.

"So, Sean tells me you guys had a little run-in last night? How you feeling?"

"It was nothing," I said.

"Sorry for coming so early, but I just wanted to make sure you were feeling better," Sean jumped in.

"Yes, I'm really okay; I don't even feel a thing," I said as convincingly as possible. Then it dawned on me. "How do you know where I live?"

"As an investigative journalist, I have my ways," he said.

"You're a journalist?" I asked.

"Yes, I'm a staff writer at a magazine in town, but I freelance, too. Your mom tells me that's something you're considering?"

He spoke slowly, in low voice, yet confidently.

"Um, for now." I glanced at Roxann.

"Actually, from your friend Peyton," he said.

I had forgotten what we were talking about; I looked at him, confused.

"I found out where you live from your friend Peyton," he said. "I looked up her number from the church contact list after you guys left last night, then I texted her and asked for your number and address. I would have called this morning, but it was too early."

"So you decided to come instead?" I asked sarcastically.

"Basically," he said, smiling at my dry sense of humor.

Surprised at how I had snapped at him, I apologized. "I'm sorry for being rude, but no need to worry about my nose."

"I had a feeling that you would say that, which is why I had to come see for myself. I hope that was alright." He kept his eyes on me the entire time he spoke, his even, soothing voice playing music in my heart. I could feel a tug each time he spoke.

"Sit down, Morgan. Come have some breakfast," Roxann said as she walked over to the stove to prepare me a plate. Sean jumped up and pulled out the chair for me. I hesitated, then sat down, still not sure of what was going on.

"So, Morgan, is there anything that I can do to help you today?"

"Not really," I said. "Why would I need help? And what could you help me with?"

"Can't you free me from all this guilt and let me make my aunt happy?"

"Uh-huh, so Mrs. Davis put you up to this?" I said.

"Not entirely, but she did suggest that I visit you today after I told her about last night—"

"Sean, I know what you can do today," Roxann chimed in. "You can tell my daughter about the crazy, unstable life of a journalist. Morgan, Sean was just telling me how he works long hours and he is always fighting for his work to be respected by others who deem the profession to be diluted and lacking credibility. Tell her," she insisted.

Roxann's enthusiasm for these details left me feeling annoyed, to say the least.

Sean must have seen the change in my expression. "Well, every career has its pros and cons. If you want, Morgan, I can tell you more about my career and answer any questions that you have."

"Actually, that would be helpful," I said. "I don't know where to begin, though. I might need some time to think about what I want to know."

"That's fine; take your time," he said. "You can always call me when you're ready."

He continued eating and I drifted off in deep thought until Roxann broke the silence, urging me to eat. Finally, Sean brought his plate over to Roxann, who was washing dishes.

"Everything was extraordinary, Ms. Ellis." He touched her gently on her shoulder and added. "I haven't had food this good since I left home."

Roxann, obviously pleased by his charm, smiled from ear to ear.

Where was his home? I wondered.

"Morgan, always a pleasure," he said with his charming smile. "And you're sure there is nothing I can do to help you today?"

Before I could answer, Roxann said, "You know I don't need you at the store today."

"Well, I have some loose ends to tie up for school and I have plans with Peyton, so—"

Sean interjected, "What about this evening? I have somewhere that I think would be great for you to visit."

I hesitated, then said, "I don't think I have any plans later."

"Okay then, it's set—Operation Feel Better About Myself is in full force."

"I'll see you later then," I said lightheartedly.

He waved to Roxann, then looked at me as he walked backward through the door.

"So, I'll pass by and get you around six. If you think of any questions, bring them, too. I'll give you the real lowdown and I won't sugarcoat anything; I promise."

"Okay, I'll see," I said.

And, just like that, Sean was in and out of my house. I pinched myself to see if I was dreaming.

Roxann raved about Sean for a good hour after he left.

"He is such a gentleman," she said. "And so handsome—I wonder if he would consider modeling in my show?"

"I don't know, Mommy. I barely know the guy."

I grabbed my shoes and my keys, then headed to Trends. Peyton insisted on me getting my hair done before my first day of school. I wanted to get it done more now, since I'd be seeing Sean later. When I walked into Trends a little before noon, the waiting area of the salon swarmed with people. I guessed that was how salons looked on Saturdays. All ten hair dryers were filled; Peyton and the other stylist seemed to have mastered a whole new level of multitasking. I waved to her and she signaled for me to come on back to the sink where she was working.

"Sharon, can you please give Morgan a relaxer when you're finished with that customer?" she asked. "She made an appointment earlier this week and I forgot to write it in the book."

I made an appointment?

"Okay, Morgan, you're up next," Sharon said. In less than fifteen minutes, I was in Sharon's chair getting my hair relaxed. I refused to make eye contact with those impatient customers waiting in the lobby. I would hate for them to ask where I came from. Forty minutes later, I was in Peyton's shampoo chair, getting my hair rinsed and washed.

"So," Peyton said.

"So what?" I asked.

"So is your nose feeling better today?"

"I've felt worse," I said.

"You will never guess who texted me last night to find out about that nose of yours," Peyton said.

"Let me guess... Could it be the boy that showed up at my house at eight-something this morning?"

"He did not!" Peyton shouted, stopping the water to look at my face.

"Yes, he did," I said. "He saw me in my too-small princess nightgown, the one Mommy made for us years ago—that you made me keep."

She laughed aloud. Everyone in the salon stared in our direction. "It's not funny," I fussed.

"Yes, it is," she said, hardly able to hold herself up. "So, what happened when he came by?"

Sidonie Walsh

"Nothing really. He hit it off with my mom. I mean, they had their own conversation brewing before I was even awake. Did you know that he's a journalist?"

"Oh, no. I actually don't know much about him other than the rumors that fly around church."

"What rumors?" I asked.

Peyton moved me to a styling chair, clipped my ends, and began putting rollers in my hair. "Well, I'm not sure how true this is, but it's what I heard. A few months ago, he moved here from Portland because he beat a policeman almost to death or something like that. Anyway, the altercation happened after the police tried to arrest him for his involvement with some gang of sorts. He's lucky, though, because I hear his dad is some big shot lawyer and got him out of jail in no time. But the condition is he has to do all these months of community service. Fortunately for him, his aunt and uncle are the pastors of Oasis, so his father convinced the judge to have him do his time there."

"Is that why he does those odd jobs at church?" I asked.

"I suppose," she said. "I hear he even has to do work for her at her house. I mean, be their little do-boy, you know, doing all their dirty work. Actually, I don't think he is pleased with it; he doesn't talk to anyone and always look pissed. I mean, last night was the first time I had heard so many words out of his mouth. And I heard that all the girls threw themselves at him when he first came. But it wasn't long before they all ran away with their feelings hurt. Nothing but a hit in the nose to get the boys attention," she joked.

"Great, I agreed to meet up with an attempted murderer later."

"Is that so?" she asked, reading way too much into my words.

"Yeah, Mommy wanted him to give me the scoop on the horrible life of a journalist. He said he has somewhere we can go, but I have no idea where."

"Oh my God! Keisha, can you polish Morgan's fingers and toes while she dries her hair?" she asked the nail technician. "My girl is going on a date!"

"I am not!"

There was no use in wasting energy on crazy Peyton. She danced as she got the next customer and brought them back to the sink.

"You go, girl!" she yelled as she passed me.

The loud sound of the dryer filled my ears. I sank in the chair, closed my eyes, and refused to be drawn into her madness.

Sean

First Staff Meeting

"The Peace in the Street Initiative is what they are calling it. Because of the excellent story, we did on the 'Journey to Area Don,' the Urban News got the news yesterday that we were given the exclusive rights to interviews to produce the story on the Initiative."

Everyone in the room clapped aloud and whistled. Barrington, the editor in chief, tried to settle them down, so he could continue. "Now, now, let us not get ahead of ourselves here. This story needs extensive research and we need someone who can put their all into it for the next several months. I need you to eat and sleep it and come up with a creative way to tell the story. We need to get to the bottom of this sudden truce that has been issued."

Everyone chimed in about the various stories that they still have working on. The murmurs grew louder and some complained about how unsafe this could be. Sean held his head low in a crouch position just listening.

And then Barrington asked, "what about you Sean? You just start, your plate not too full and from what I hear from over at News Time, you are quite the researcher. You think you up for the challenge?"

The question was unexpected for Sean. Where he came from people would be fighting to take on a high visibility story like this. "Ah... yeah... sure, why not," he said. And just like that Sean got assigned to the story that no one wanted.

They assigned Tameka Porter, one of the staff writers that helped in the last story of the area dons, to assist and get him up to speed. Sean thought she was a pretty girl, nice figure and dressed well. Her makeup was always on point and most of their time driving across town, she spent it reapplying lip gloss and fixing something on herself in the mirror. But she knew her stuff. For the first few months that Sean worked with her she insisted that he had to learn the soul of the people in various parts of the city.

She took him to many ghetto areas from Tivoli Gardens, Denham Town, Water House, Seaview and Maxfield Avenue. They hung out with the people on the corner sometimes, exchanging stories, now and then they would bring them some patties, cigarettes or for a drink give them a few dollars or a smalls as they would say when asking. "Sean, beg you a smalls nuh?"

After a while, aside from a few beyond help degenerates, Sean noticed that regardless of the party, the majority of the people were the same. They were oppressed and wanted help. They craved to be heard and considered because they needed more help than the promises of quality roads to drive on.

"Mi need a way to feed mi pickney dem tonight," one lady said with anger in her voice and tears in her eyes.

It was clear to Sean where the Politian's found their niche. The peoples' level of desperation made them easy targets for bribes. They were ready to give their vote to the promise of something directly affecting them. On several occasion, Sean saw people pulling up with a van back filled with food and fruits, compliments of a Politian. Some of them had their lights, water and cable always on and no bill ever came. A cycle that seemed to be only broken when it's time for a change in power. Everyone fought super hard to keep or to take back what they can get.

Chapter 7

A loud roar vibrated through the house and I ran to look through my bedroom window. His black car stopped inches away from Roxann's fountain in my front yard. *Oh my God, this cannot be good.* My heart was racing so fast. Not just because of Peyton's revelation about Sean's rumored messy past, but because of how he makes me feel. I squirmed at the thought of those giddy girls back in high school *oohing* and *aahing* over him.

I had spent the last two hours getting ready. I must have changed ten times. I had picked up his aunt's business card a few times, tempted to call him. I wanted to know how to dress—or maybe to cancel; I couldn't decide which.

I looked in the mirror at my bubbling curls, realizing now that Peyton definitely had cut my hair instead of clipping it as she claimed. Sean had seen me this morning looking far less than perfect and I would hate for him to think I was trying too hard to look nice for him. With one swoop, I butchered Peyton's creation by pulling my hair into a ponytail.

It was 6:10 pm, Sean was outside, and I was still in my robe. *I have no idea what to wear!* I heard voices outside and peeped through my window. Sean was talking to Tony, apparently discussing something about his car because Tony made hand gestures towards it.

Sean had on khaki slacks and a long-sleeved plaid shirt. He wasn't too dressy, but not exactly casual, either. I walked into my closet a lot more confidently than I had all day. I quickly got dressed in fitted grey skirt with a puffed-sleeve white blouse and a wide, black patent leather belt and matching sling-back wedges. I loosened my hair, leaving it out to sway and bounce with the wind as Peyton had intended. I took one last look in the mirror. The slight swelling of my nose had gone and I barely felt any pain. I grabbed a note pad and pen, threw them in my bag, and walked outside to meet Sean.

I could hear Tony telling him he'd go get me as he gave Sean a business card.

"No need," I said from behind him.

"There you are," he said.

He glanced at Sean. "I don't know what's with these girls, always having their dates wait."

I could not believe he said that—out loud, out of his mouth!

"This is not a date," I quickly replied.

"Oh, it's not? My apologies," he said, obviously having fun at my expense and not buying a thing I just said.

"So where are you guys going?" he asked.

I hesitated, then said, "I'm not sure."

I looked at Sean for an answer. He'd had a playful smile on his face the entire time. He leaned off his car, opened my door, and said to Tony, "We are going on an educational adventure."

"Alright, Morgan, pay attention," Tony said, laughing as he walked into the house.

Sean walked around his side of the car, looked at me, and said, "Nice guy."

"He's a pain in the rear end, that's what he is."

Sean started the car and we drove off with a world of noise following behind us.

"So where are we really going? I asked after we had driven a few minutes.

"To work," he answered.

"To work?" I asked, confused.

"Well, I'm working and you're coming along for the ride," he said, smiling.

I think he got pleasure from my frazzled states. Whenever I'm confused or uncomfortable, he would get this smirk on his face. I collected myself and asked him, "So where do you work?"

"*Urban News*," he answered, very casually, like I should know it.

"*Urban News*? I've never heard of it," I said.

"It's a political news magazine company off Red Hills Road."

"Oh, okay. So why exactly am I going with you?"

"A day in the life, you know," he said, smiling again.

"I guess," I said skeptically.

"Tonight, I'm actually taking you to a debate," he said.

"Who's debating?"

"The Right Honorable Desmond Porter and Peter Willis," he said casually.

"You mean we're going to a debate between the prime minister and the opposition leader?"

Surprised, I leaned forward in my seat and looked at him. Up close he was breathtaking—literally! He, too, had gotten himself cleaned up since this morning. His face was freshly shaved and smooth, his hair low and well-defined, just like the first time I saw him. I sat back in my chair, a helpless feeling taking over me.

"Are you okay?" he asked.

"I'm fine," I said quickly.

"You sure?" he asked again. "You're not in pain or anything?"

When I didn't answer him right away, he said, "Your nose doesn't hurt anymore, right?"

I wish that's where I hurt, I thought.

"Of course not! I'm okay, really."

We pulled up to a stoplight; I took a deep breath and composed my thoughts. I found myself doing that a lot around this boy.

"How exactly did you get invited to the prime minister's debate? Isn't it reserved for specific groups of people?"

"Yes, like the media," he said calmly.

"Duh, I knew that," I said, a little embarrassed for missing the obvious.

"So, I'll be working and you'll be learning," he said.

Reaching over me, he opened the glove compartment, handed me a name badge attached to a lanyard, and said, "Here…you have to wear this in."

"Tameka Porter—who's she?"

"You," he said laughing. Finally, he said, "It belongs to my coworker."

"Oh great, I'm breaking in now? What if I get caught?"

"You won't. They don't really look at those things," he said. "Just stay right behind me in the line and do what I do."

We approach the gate leading to auditorium where the debate was being held. The line to get in was long and I felt a tad bit nervous. All the various news outlets were on the scene with cars and people everywhere.

A few stragglers with their signs lined the gate to the entrance. *Persistent,* I thought. Sean had his elbow folded out his car window and nodded to a few people as he passed by. As we were about to go through the gate, I heard a lady say, "What a gwaan, Sean?"

"Nuttin mi deh yah, you alright?"

"Yeah, man, mi cool."

We drove through the gate and I wondered how he knew these people. I didn't ask and he didn't say. A parking attendant with orange wands in his hands approached the car. Sean showed his badge and he directed us to the media parking. We parked between a *Channel 7/TVJ* van and a *Kingston Times* van.

We got out the car. Sean reached in the back for a brown tie and tied it around his neck. He pushed his shirt into his pants and reached in the back again, this time for a brown blazer. Just like that, he transformed from business casual to all business. Words could not describe how great he looked and the confidence that went along with his attire was refreshing.

I looked away, trying to act as naturally as possible. Then it occurred to me. *I wonder if I'm dressed up enough.* I glanced over to where Sean was still fixing his tie. Our eyes met and he smiled that sly smile that he had started to display openly.

He said, "Not everyone can look as stunning as you, Morgan. Some of us have to work at it."

And, just like that, all my worries vanished. I blushed and my heart went to the high heavens and back.

People scurried by Sean's car, carrying ID cards from all over the island. We saw three ladies from the *Jamaica Observer*, another set from *The Gleaner,* and many more people with names I did not recognize, who must be from rural papers. Sean hung his ID around his neck and signaled for me to put on mine, claiming my new name for the night.

"Are you ready to go in, Tameka?" he asked jokingly.

I smiled and, walking alongside him, blended into the crowd heading towards the entrance.

At the gate, more people lined the fence to the National Arena, where the first of many debates around the island would take place. In three months, our country would decide its fate. We would either stick with PNP's leader Desmond Porter or bring on his opponent, JLP's Peter Willis. Either way, it didn't matter to me. I had never voted before, though I will have a chance this year, since my birthday is a few weeks before Election Day.

The big beige building stretched high and wide before us. Big, bright, round lights illuminated the grounds. Flags from various countries lined the side of the building and hung above our heads. The line moved quickly. Everyone seemed professional and obviously had their missions set.

Sean reached out his hand for mine. "Stay close," he said.

I held his hand and walked close behind him. His hand was strong yet gentle. He maneuvered his way through the crowd, bringing me along with him the entire time. We got to the front, where he lifted his name badge from his neck and showed the guard at the entrance. The guard took a few seconds to look at the badge, then at Sean, and then sent him through the metal detector. Sean released my hand and walked through.

Now it was my turn. My heart beat faster as I was left alone to face the embarrassment. *Sure I can pass for this girl.* She was about my complexion and her hair was down in the picture, hiding the contours of her face.

"Hello," I said as I approached the guard.

I lifted my badge for him to see. He looked at me, then at the picture, then at the picture again. He took a few seconds too long, convincing me that he would throw me out the line. I glanced over at Sean, waiting for me on the other side. He smiled and winked; my heart melted. I forgot to be nervous. Then the guard looked up and sent me through.

Reunited with Sean, I relaxed. He smiled. "See? That wasn't so bad."

"I'm fine now. But I was sure he was about to tell me to step out the line."

He laughed. "Would I let that happen to you? Don't worry; they barely look at those things."

"Oh no, he looked," I said.

"Are you sure he wasn't just looking at you?"

He asked this question with a composed voice, looking straight into my eyes. I had a hard time finding words. He was too gorgeous and, for some reason, I would bet he knows it.

"Yes, I'm sure," I said. "He was staring at Tameka Porter."

We both laughed as we turned the corner into a large room filled with people. Sean turned left, leading the way to the side of the room. He stopped at the area filled with media representatives from all over the island. They all had their tape recorders and notepads in hand.

The ones from the TV stations had microphones in hand and people in front of them adjusting cameras.

We walked behind them and found two seats in the second row. I could hear introductions from the TV reporters all around me. The loud words sounded almost like a song being sung in rounds. Their melodious voices were as intriguing as their appearances. We sat close to one reporter as the cameraman counted down to her cue to start. The curls in her low hair stayed in place, her makeup appeared flawless, and she looked exquisite in a beautiful purple dress. I watch intently as she began,

"In about fifteen minutes, Prime Minister Desmond Porter and opposition leader Peter Willis are scheduled to take part in an hour-long debate here at the National Arena. If you look behind me, hundreds of people have gathered to witness the first of three debates around the Island. Icebreaker topics that are said to be addressed tonight include the island's irrepressible crime and violence, plans for a stronger economy, and amendments to the country's policies and procedures. One hot issue is the rolling election date now in place, with no set date for the election, but one that is chosen by the prime minister a few months before election. In a few weeks there will be the JLP rally in Montego Bay's Sam Sharpe Square and a PNP rally in

Kingston's Half Way Tree Square. We will bring you the dates and the times for the upcoming rallies in the coming weeks. Stay tuned, CVM will bring you the entire debate in just a few minutes. This is Rachel Lawson, reporting live from downtown Kingston."

I knew she sounded and looked familiar. I couldn't believe it was Rachel Lawson. I watched her some evenings and I had always admired her style and eloquence. I looked out into the crowd congregating in the center of the room. The audience, unlike the stragglers outside, all wore suits and appeared to represent the upper and middle-classes in the country. Everyone mingled openly. Though the room was filled to capacity, it was orderly—nothing like what had been going on in the street.

The room grew quieter as everyone sat down in preparation for the start of the night's debate. A feeling of excitement came over me. I turned to Sean, who had his recorder, notepad, and pen in hand, scribbling away.

He looked up, giving me a half smile and asked, "Having fun yet?"

I shook my head with a big smile on my face. "Should I be doing something?"

"It's up to you," he said. "I just want you to enjoy this experience. I certainly don't want to put you to work."

With that decided, I placed my hand on my chin and anxiously waited for the start.

Sean chuckled, probably because I hadn't argued when he told me to not do any work. I knew I was too fascinated; I wouldn't be composed enough to do anything that made sense anyway.

The chattering around us subsided until every sound was deliberate. The camera people had their lenses focused on the stage while others prepped their recorders. I sat there, observing everyone's dedication as they anxiously waited for the start. I'm not sure what, but I felt something in the air. I felt at peace inside; I felt happy, almost like having a good dream with Sean right next to me.

A week ago, I could never have imagined being in his presence and now I was sitting next to him. There was also something surreal being a part of and observing life in their world, the journalists' world. Not just witnessing the product on screen, but also watching it all come together. It intrigued me. I could see myself being that person behind the scenes. I could see myself as the person with the pen, the one who develops the story and presents it for all to see.

On the stage, a heavyset woman in a bright blue skirt and a white jacket took a seat in the left corner of the stage. She had a microphone and began speaking:

"Good evening, ladies and gentlemen. I am Yvette McFarlane from the Center of Literacy and Education and I will be your host tonight. I want to welcome you all to the first of three debates between Prime Minister Desmond Porter and opposition leader Peter Willis. The purpose of these debates is to bring each party's views and plans for the country to the people. Let's bring them out before I go over the rules and guidelines for this evening."

She announced them both at the same time and they walked on the stage together, waving to the crowd. Desmond Porter, a tall man with horrible posture, wore a black suit with an orange tie. Peter Willis, though also tall, had a stocky build and wore a green tie.

Everyone rose to their feet, clapped, and whistled. They held up their different banners and signs, waving them high in the air. Afraid of blowing out my eardrums, I plugged my ears with my fingers.

Sean laughed at this and said something to me that I couldn't make out. He clapped along with everyone around us.

The noise subsided. Yvette McFarland, after shaking both their hands, gave the speakers the rules for the night. They would have three minutes to answer each question and one minute for rebuttals.

She began, "Prime Minister Porter, the first question goes to you. The country's crime rate is skyrocketing and offenders seemingly running rampant around the country; what would you say is the cause of this and what are your plans to counter these?"

"Yvette, sorry for the early correction, but I want to point out that the crime rate has actually decreased 2.6% since I've taken office. The notion that it is rising is just a perception because I think the people of this country are weary and rightfully so. We have efforts in place to expose those who are causing this uproar to our communities and hurting innocent citizens. The majority of the people of Jamaica are upstanding law-abiding citizens who are hardworking and resourceful. However, a few believe that they are above the law. They feel that they are indestructible and I have news for them."

He looked in the camera as if talking directly to the few.

"There is a saying that the small fox spoils the vine. The vine will not be broken, but we will seek and bring down the parasites that are responsible for the misfortunes of this country and its people."

Some of his supporters clapped and waved their banners, but the cheering was short-lived as Yvette regained control of the debate. I looked over at Sean, who was busy writing. Actually, it looked like he was sketching something. I tried to make it out, but Yvette asked Peter Willis for his response, drawing my attention back to the stage.

"My fellow Jamaicans, the Prime Minister is right in saying the vine will not be broken, but not if he has anything to do with it. How much time will we give him to work up the guts to do what he's been saying for years? Has anyone ever wondered what these plans are that he has in place? I, like you, have been waiting for these plans for years and they have not come to fruition. We've given him chance after chance and now it's time for a new leader to, once and for all, put a stop to this country's crimes. We need to put some fear in these offenders' hearts and make examples of the leaders of these groups in order to eliminate the crime epidemic. We need to take the appropriate steps geared to infuse life back into the country's economy. Greater emphasis should be placed on education and assistance for the poor. This will essentially alleviate the struggle which will in turn reduce the crime and violence on our citizens."

When he finished, a burst of excitement filled the room, with the majority of the audience jumping to their feet and clapping aloud for the opposition leader.

Everyone around me had almost shocked looks on their faces. Peter Willis was the clear favorite; the crowd's response set the stage for the entire evening. Peter Willis and the audience at large met everything Desmond Porter said with cynicism. Even Porter's supporters seemed unsure when clapping for him. Peter Willis, on the other hand, received one standing ovation after another.

Credibility is a powerful a thing. After a while, it didn't matter what they said. It didn't matter how smooth and confident Desmond Porter sounded. It didn't matter that Peter Willis sounded crass and unpolished and looked sloppy. For the people in the room, all the right answers came out of his mouth and only lies came out of Desmond Porter's.

I felt sorry for him and looked away. Sean, noticing my dismayed expression and asked if I was okay. I smiled, of course, and told him I was fine. I still had no idea why these public exchanges made me uneasy. It might have to do with me not liking embarrassing situations or something else. Something more practical and easier to explain, but nothing came to me. I just sat there cringing with every loud outburst that followed.

Chapter 8

I woke up early to Roxann's *Sunday Morning Joy* on RJR radio station. The sound of Roxann singing loudly along with Grace Thrillers beat at my door. For someone who doesn't go to church, she really loved gospel music. Grandma Lilith told me that my mom had been a great singer when she was young. She used to lead all the songs for the choir and she wrote quite a few, too.

I found that very hard to believe. Roxann always put her career first; when it came to God and helping the needy, she always said, "God helps those who help themselves." She had no pity for the deprived. She often scolded me for giving money to the people begging at the side of the road.

"You know that you're supporting a habit. You know what would happen if you and everyone else would stop giving them handouts?"

She would ask, but I knew better than to answer. She had her own answer.

"They would go and find jobs—a job is a job, you know. You can't be picky when you are hungry. Instead they use this as their job and all you blinking idiots are their employers."

On Sundays though, Roxann turned up her music and sang aloud. I think back to what Grandma Lilith had said and wondered when she changed. Meanwhile, I covered my head and tried to fall back asleep, but it was no use. As soon as I realized I was fully awake, my mind switched to Sean and last night.

We had left a few minutes before the debate ended in order to beat the traffic. Even as we navigated the crowd, I wondered why my mood changed, why I felt so somber. As we were walking to his car, Sean asked, "You weren't interested, were you?"

"Oh no, it was very interesting! I really enjoyed myself and I learned a lot."

"Oh really? And what did you learn?"

Not knowing exactly what I really wanted to convey, I said, "the state of the country and the plans to build it up strong again."

He laughed as he opened my door.

As I sat down, waiting for him to come around to his seat, remaining composed and confident. I refused to wonder what his laughter did or did not mean. He got in, closed the door, started the engine, and began reversing. Some other people were leaving, too, but not many. Like when we entered, a few loiterers still leaned against the fence. Sean tapped his horn twice as we drove by them.

The road ahead was clear and the night calm. Over the loud noise of his car, he said, "Now, for real, what did you think of tonight?"

He looked at me with his intense stare that melted my heart and any stubbornness that might have been there. I opened my mouth; the thoughts that came out surprised even me.

"I did learn something about the people, at least the seemingly upper and middle-class Jamaicans present tonight. One of my theories is that the people really crave change. I get that...I really do, because the country has been in this slump for so long. But what I guess I had a problem with..." I stopped talking and started to think.

What did I have a problem with? I haven't had a chance to think this through; something bothered me in there, but what? Why does it matter that they were bashing a politician who misled the people for so many years and who made the people of this country lose hope? I don't know...

I almost forgot that I was in the car with Sean having a conversation. Finally, he looked over to me and said, "So you have a problem with...?"

"What?" I asked, clearly not mentally present.

"You were saying what you had a problem with something."

"I'm not sure, but I think it has to do with things being so bad that people think anything is an improvement. There was something thought-provoking and ominous in that room tonight that screams manipulation. Something off—am I making any sense?" I asked, buying myself time to figure out what I actually wanted to say.

He had that look on his face, the same one he'd had when waiting for his aunt in Roxann's store. He wasn't just deep in thought, but piecing something together.

After a beat, he said, "Go on."

He sounded encouraging and his face looked friendly. I opened my mouth to go on, not knowing if I would find the right words to sum it all up.

"How can I put this…? I know," I said. The passion that I felt came alive. My sudden confidence surprised even me. I turned toward him, gesturing to paint the picture for him.

"It's like a football game. Both teams show up; one team came to play but the other team knows it has already won. I'm sure that's not unusual, the teams should feel confident. However, the twist is that the crowd seems to know the score, too—and so does the referee, before anyone even comes to the game. Everyone except the team that came to play knows this information. I feel bad for the team that came to play," I finally said.

He pulled up to the stoplight and gave me a weird look. Maybe he was confused, but he didn't ask me to clarify. With the same pensive look on his face, he said, "And I guess the question is how did the other players know that they won before starting to play? And how did the referee and the people in the stands know?

Something more than confidence, more like fraudulent play?" He looked at me.

I didn't answer because his question sounded rhetorical. I sat stiffly in my seat, giving him my own puzzled look. I turned away with mixed feelings, insecure about what I had said. I mean, I didn't think my feelings had any merit. *What do I know? I am a lowly seventeen-year-old without any real-world experience making comments about age-old norms.*

I preferred to think about the way I felt as he spoke, a new feeling for me. I kept my eyes on Sean's hand gliding on the steering wheel as he left the stoplight. If a heart could smile, my heart was smiling. He had seriously analyzed my comparison, pulling truths out of what I said. He had made no concessions and did not seem amused by my outlook. He hadn't try telling me the ways of the world or considered my views infantile. He took my observations as facts and asked meaningful questions about my naive thoughts.

"I'm trying to sleep here, turn down the music!" Tony yelled down the stairs at Roxann. Her music blasted even louder, competing with the drilling sound of her sewing machine. Already up, I walked over to my window seat and listened as the music bellowed,

> *Don't try to tell me God is dead*
> *He woke me up this Morning,*

Don't try to tell me my God is dead
He lives within my heart,
He opened up my blinded eyes
And set me on my way,
So don't try to tell me that my God is dead
I just spoke to Him today.

I looked at the fountain below and followed the water's continuous flow. I felt the closest thing to tranquility that I'd felt since my summer in the country. Bands of water squirted wide in the air before falling back into the fountain, only to start again. The order and splendor reminded me of the beauty in the country, the cloud clusters at the top of the mountain, the glowing sky as the sun rises, and the rooster singing at the breaking of the dawn. I soaked up the moment and reflected.

My life as I knew it was changing before my very eyes. After an uneventful last few months, it was gaining momentum. I felt a stirring in my spirit, like something was brewing. A feeling screamed, *You should have enjoyed boredom while you had the chance because life is changing*.

I would start my first day as a college student in the morning. I would go to classes between nine and one, Monday through Thursday. I wondered what I would do with all my spare time. *Maybe I should get a job, a real job*. Then I remembered how Roxann said that college was not easy and I didn't need to work right now—unless I was helping out at her store, of course. Then there was Sean, who was there, but not really there—I knew absolutely nothing about him, but he left me wanting more.

Roxann must have lowered her music and closed the door to her sewing room because the volume of both the music and her machine faded.

I gazed out the window, not sure what I was looking for. I knew I prayed for lucidity and guidance from God. I knew I wanted to find myself in all the shuffles of my life, before my spirit ended up crushed. *When did I—I mean, my core self—disappear in my own life?* I felt like I lived for everyone but me. I think sharing my ideas with Sean last night and the way he nurtured my thoughts stirred up something in me. It reminded me of my dreams; the ones that I had tucked far away.

A feeling of anxiety ran through my body and I began to cry. *When did this change? When did my thoughts stop mattering? When did I start caring so much about pleasing people?* When I was young, my grandmother would tell my parents, "She has a mouth on her." Back then, I expressed myself in every way with passion at the core. I had an opinion about everything and someone would hear about it.

With one chapter in my life closing and another one starting, I didn't feel that I had been true to myself in the closing chapter. I wanted to go back and fix some things. I wanted to infuse some of me in each line, but it was too late.

When Sean dropped me off at home last night, he had said, "You know, Morgan, you might just be onto something."

"I doubt it," I said as I closed the car door. "It was just some silly feeling; I'm sure it was nothing."

"Well, we'll see. Some of the best findings start with a hunch or a feeling," he said effortlessly.

As he put his car in gear to leave, he said, "You are very intuitive; don't ever lose sight of that. What's your last name, by the way?"

"Ellis," I responded, "why?"

"No reason. I just want to get closer to the complete picture."

I hope my face didn't give my confusion away. Without thinking, I asked, "What's yours?"

"Squire," he answered.

"Sean Squire—it has a nice ring to it."

He smiled. "Well, Morgan Ellis, you gave me a lot to think about. See you around."

"Bye—thanks for inviting me, by the way. It was great."

"We have to do it again, then," he said, revving his engine without moving.

I felt his stare as I walked towards my house and opened the door. I heard the loud roar of his car and knew he was gone.

A loud knock on my door startled me. Snapped out of my thoughts of Sean, I jumped to my feet. I dried my tears as I climbed into my bed, pretending to still be asleep.

Roxann opened the door, "You up?"

I rolled over slowly. "I am now."

Quietly, she said, "I didn't hear you come in last night. What did you guys do?"

"We went to that debate," I said absentmindedly.

"What debate?"

"The debate with Peter Willis and Desmond Porter."

"I didn't know that young man was taking you somewhere dangerous!" she said with her eyebrows all knitted up.

"It wasn't dangerous, Mom. It was held at the arena with the 'who's who' of the island attending."

"Oh. So what did you think?" she asked.

I realized I had to downplay my interest and hold back from displaying any journalistic insights, so I did.

"It was silly and manipulative and…a waste of time," I finally said.

"I know—I keep telling you journalism is tough and all about money-making. The media are forced into unsafe situations and swayed to report the way the people footing the bills want them to."

"Yeah, I can see that," I said.

Every word that my mother said was true, but that was exactly why I wanted to do this. I want to change the way people perceived the media. I wanted to be the one who told the truth, but I know she wouldn't understand.

Roxann had one-sided views, practical and realistic with no ounce of fantasy in the mix. Everything had to make sense in her head or she deemed it wrong in some way. In her mind, the world was not a playground, no bubble that would protect you, and idealistic viewpoints needed to be quickly dismissed. My mother could only see things her way.

To avoid an argument, I said, "You're right. That's exactly how it was."

"You see? I'm happy that you recognize it now for what it truly is." Satisfied, Roxann stepped out and closed my door. I looked at the ceiling, wishing I could have been true to my feelings.

Chapter 9

October

"The story has to pull out the reader's human emotions. It has to reach its audience in a relevant way. They should not have to ask the question, *why do I care?* That emotion should be there, seamless; it should rise to the surface and stir up such explicit feelings that the reader connects to the story as their own, which ultimately leads to action," said Professor Logan.

She thought it important to tell us, with as much time as possible, about our final assignment for Journalism 101. The semester had just started, but in eleven weeks it would be over. I needed to write a poignant story, but I knew of nothing emotional going on.

Over the past couple of weeks, I'd been going through the motions of adjusting to school and keeping up with homework. *Oh, there is so much homework!* I always had something to do.

My English literature professor, Mr. Luscher, assigned several books that we needed to read. For some reason, all the books were about vampires. He knew a lot about all the different kinds of vampires, though he came across as pretty normal. He even looked like a typical professor. *Where did his obsession with vampires come from? What would make a person use something like vampire literature as the core subject matter of his entire syllabus?*

I had decided there was definitely something abnormal about college professors. If they weren't hippies, they were vampire lovers or extremely rigid.

In the middle of a lecture, my Law and Ethics professor informed us that he did not pass cars on a highway. He stayed in one lane for the entire ride, until he was about to exit. I could not imagine how someone could stay in just one lane in Kingston traffic. How long did it take him to get to his destination?

With carefully thought-out logic, he explained that, "The lanes all move equally, just at different times. By being patient and respecting the order, everyone will eventually move at the same rate."

I thought that was very admirable or crazy, but that was his take on it, as he discussed it in ethics. He left me a little perplexed. *Is it unethical when I switch lanes and move with the flow of traffic?* I smiled as I thought about Roxann; in that case, she would be ruled unethical for sure!

I snapped out of my thoughts as Ms. Logan greeted the guest who had just come into the class. On the first day, she had told us that one of her past students would be stopping by to talk about ideas for our final project.

Yet never would I have imagined who would be standing in front of the class that day.

I hadn't seen Sean since he took me home after the debate. I couldn't say the same thing about my thoughts and dreams; I saw him there constantly. I had even thought about asking Peyton if we could go to Oasis tomorrow night to see him. But here he stood, in my class. He looked nice in gray slacks, a green shirt, and a skinny striped tie. He took off his messenger bag as he sat in a chair next to Ms. Logan.

I noticed all the girls paying close attention, whispering and giggling as Sean and Ms. Logan made small talk up front. One girl got up and walked slowly across the front of the room, staring at him as she passed. He glanced up, but quickly returned to his conversation with Ms. Logan. I sat there, half disgusted and half puzzled.

"May I have your attention, class?" Ms. Logan started. "I would like to introduce to everyone my special guest today, Sean Squire. Among other things, Sean works at the local magazine, *Urban News*. I'm going to embarrass Sean a bit today," she said, smiling.

He smiled back, though he looked uncomfortable.

"Sean was one of my best students," she said giddily. Her hippy hair and big glasses almost completely covered her face, her loose clothes draped awkwardly, and her bangles made a ringing sound as she gestured to him.

"I have to say Sean's biggest asset is his passion for research. He needs to reach the bottom, the true basis of every story. I think he will provide you with excellent guidance on your projects and how to research them. Please write down any story ideas that you may have and, while we have him, use Sean to guide you in the right direction."

She signaled for Sean to come up. As he walked to the front of the class, she said, "Oh, by the way, one lucky student will have a chance to shadow Sean at the *Urban News* for one whole day. I will tell you more about how we will decide who that student will be, after Sean finishes speaking."

I watched him walk to the front; I had never seen anyone more handsome. My heart beat in my throat and I waited attentively, eager to hear his every word.

"Well, thank you, Ms. Logan, for that wonderful intro. Ms. Logan was right when she said that the foundation of every story is passion and research. It's imperative to strip the façade off each and every story—and they each have a façade."

He grabbed the room's television and quickly rolled it to the middle of the class. He turned it around so the back of the TV faced the class.

"You all are no longer in front of the TV, but behind it. You will be responsible for the news and stories that touch the world. You are expected to tell the truth, the whole truth, and nothing but the truth," he said, smiling. "That, in itself, is a daunting task, but more than that, it is an important role. But how do you get to that truth? Research," he said. "In every story, you have to assume that there is more than what meets the eye. It's almost like being a detective, challenging everything you see and hear. Digging to find the truth is your responsibility, almost your right and duty, as a journalist. Finding the human touches makes the story relevant. Research is the way to do both. Research not only brings out a story, but it brings out the real story."

He pushed the TV back in place, saying, "I was reminded of that recently…" He paused as his gaze fell on me.

Staring, he said nothing for a moment. Everyone started turning in the direction of his gaze. I turned, too. He must have just spotted me in the class. I smiled slightly at his disorientation. Then he continued like a pro, before anyone could tell who he had seen.

"I was reminded of the importance of transparency and curiosity in a journalist's eyes from my little cousin, who is a new college student. She accompanied me to the prime minister's debate the other day."

I laughed inside.

"Because of those qualities, she asked some important questions that every journalist should ask. The biggest assets you have as new journalists are your uncontaminated viewpoints and your gut feelings. You should make those work for you."

He looked my way with his sly one-sided smile before continuing.

"Well, I'm very excited for all of you who will join me in this rewarding career. It is not all fun and games, but, at the end of the day, you will rest easy knowing that you are a teller of truth."

He paused and stuck his hands in his pockets. All eyes were on him. "Any questions?"

A few people put their hands up, presenting ideas for their final projects and asking him for suggestions. Two girls asked how they could be the lucky student to shadow him for a day. Ms. Logan quickly chimed in, "Now, now, students. To make this fair, Sean will choose who the student will be."

She handed him a stack of papers and asked him to take a seat.

She turned to us. "I've handed Sean the papers that you wrote the first day of class, the paper on why you want to be journalists. He will read these papers while you take a break. By the end of class, Sean will announce the lucky winner."

On the island, rain is as sure as the constant sunshine. It poured on and off all day Friday, which made Roxann unhappy. With just eight days until her fashion show, she needed to have her final fitting for her models. Thanks to the rain, all fifteen models crowded into Roxann's sewing room and, thanks to the constant stream of wet shoes in the house, I spent most of the day wiping and re-wiping the floors.

Roxann, her face stern, moved steadily, pinning and adjusting garments on the models. Peyton helped with their hairs, while Lisa from the store picked out their makeup. I kept busy playing hostess, replenishing fruits and snacks, and directing people to the restroom.

The day was tiring. I was happy when the rain stopped and most of the models left. I peeked into Roxann's sewing room to check the progress; only two girls remained. I closed the door, relieved, and began packing up the food and getting the house back in order.

I could hear Peyton laughing outside on the patio. I peeped through the window and, sure enough, Tony was out there with her. Peyton, relaxed on a lawn chair and Tony propped himself up in the chair next to her, enthusiastically telling a story. She giggled as he complained about how miserable Roxann had been all day.

Earlier today, in her anxious rage, she had shouted at Tony to hurry up and help her move the table to the other side of the living room. Considering that he had been up since seven on a Saturday morning helping her on the road, Tony had gotten frustrated with her tone, thrown the ice he was carrying into the cooler, and shouted for her to wait.

"I can only do one thing at a time!" he had snapped.

I smiled at his telling of the story and he spotted me at the window and mimicked the look he often does when ridiculing Roxann. I chuckled, but kept it low because I knew better. Roxann had a way of getting worked up when stressed. I knew to stay out of her way and do as she said when she got in one of her moods.

She would bark out orders and cuss at everyone and everything, even mother nature herself.

"You would have to do this today, right?" she gestured at the rainy sky.

On the patio, Peyton and Tony grew silent. I looked again; they were staring at each other. Peyton nervously turned away, twitching and fixing her hair. I stepped away from the window and went upstairs to relax. I couldn't help feeling that their silence spoke louder than words. I left them alone to enjoy their weird little moment.

Sean still lingered on my mind. He wasn't the only reason I wanted to go to Oasis that night, but he was a big part of it.

We decide to go. Since Peyton was already at my house, she got dressed from my closet, as usual. She wore a short white skirt, one that I've worn at the beach before. She put a snug orange shirt with it, finishing her look with her five-inch orange platforms. Her hair this week, a copper-colored curly weave, complimented her attire in a way that only Peyton could manage. I smiled and gave her the thumbs-up. In her realm, it worked for her. To see Peyton in something conventional would be like seeing a dog talk. It would not seem right.

I, on the other hand, wore a long, green linen skirt with a fitted black top and a high black strappy sandal. I did my hair in a tight ponytail, since I hadn't had time to have it washed all day.

Night and day, that was me and Peyton, but for some reason our differences worked well together.

When we got downstairs and went outside, Tony was filling my car with Roxann's stuff, including plants from the house she wanted delivered to the party planner for next week's fashion show, boxes of platters and utensils, and only God knows what else.

"What are you doing?" I asked him, annoyed.

"Ask your mother—she wanted me to pack these in your car so she can drop them off tomorrow."

"What about her car?" I complained.

"Full," he said, pointing to her car, overflowing with boxes of its own.

"What about your car?" I asked.

He stared at me with a look that said, *Are you for real?*

I really should have bought my own car like he had, then Roxann's need to fill it with junk at a moment's notice would not be an issue.

"How are we going to get to church now?" I asked.

"I'll take you guys," Tony said, looking at Peyton.

As if he spoke to her heart, she said, "How about you take us and stay? I mean, you can come if you want; you might enjoy yourself." She looked away nervously.

"Hmm," he said, considering.

I hoped my face did not show what I was thinking. *These two got it bad.*

He finally said, "Naw, I don't think so. I actually wanted to see that Jackie Chan movie coming out tonight."

Peyton's face lit up, then dropped.

"I wanted to see that movie, too," she whined.

"Then come," Tony said casually.

"How about we make a deal?" Peyton asked. "You come to church with us and we will be done by nine-thirty or so. Then we can go with you afterwards. Right, Morgan?"

"I don't know about that part, but, Tony, you should come with us," I said, walking over to his car.

It didn't take much convincing. Before long, he ran upstairs, changed his t-shirt for a white collared shirt, and left with us for Oasis.

Chapter 10

It had been about an hour since we arrived at church. All the gadgets had been put away and the lights were finally on. Tony seemed to have found the whole thing extremely entertaining. He didn't seem shocked or unsettled like I had been when I first came to Oasis. He smiled at the disco lights and fake smoke that filled the air. He even commented on the excellent sound system and he had danced the entire time. Peyton and I laughed at his comedic talents, glad that he was having fun.

The door swung open several times throughout the night, but no Sean. I was tempted to go check outside or in the kitchen to see if I could find him, but wasn't brave enough. Peyton waved to redbone Eric and his friend Bones, talking to a group of people on the other side of the room. She didn't go over to them, but stayed with Tony instead.

Mrs. Davis walked towards us from her office; her bright smile leading the way. "Morgan, Peyton, it is so great seeing you girls!"

We got up together and she smothered us both with a big, tight squeeze. "And who, may I ask, is this handsome young man?"

"This is my big brother, Anthony," I said.

Peyton chimed in. "He's our chauffeur tonight and we convinced him to wait inside."

We all laughed.

"I'm really happy I did; it's very nice to meet you, Mrs. Davis."

"The pleasure is all mine," she said, squeezing his hands. "Well, I'll catch up with you children later."

As she walked off, she stopped and asked, "You guys didn't happen to see my nephew anywhere, did you?"

"No, I haven't," I answered.

And then I couldn't help asking, "Is he here?"

"He was, but I asked him to go back home because I left my glasses. He should have been back by now, though."

Tony went over to help the guys rearrange the chairs. I followed Peyton's gaze to him; he was talking to a girl. He obviously knew her as they talked energetically.

"Tony with one of his girls," I said without thinking.

Peyton's expression changed. She turned nonchalantly, then suddenly said, "I'll be right back."

She walked over to redbone Eric and gave him a hug, clearly to get Tony's attention. She laughed loudly, engaged in a conversation that I'm sure she devised. It seemed to work; I caught Tony staring at her as he walked towards me.

I scanned the room; still no Sean. I felt a little anxious and tried to calm myself down. *Why do I want to see him so badly anyway? It's not as if I have a grand master plan of what to say or do. It's probably for the best that he isn't here.*

Peyton and Tony came back to sit next to me for the second half of the Oasis meeting. Peyton was a little quieter that her normal self, probably because of Tony. He sat at the edge of his chair and asked what would happen next in the meeting. I explained to him that the show was over; this part went more like a traditional youth meeting. He seemed bored by my explanation and gave me a fake yawn. Peyton would typically laugh at that, but nothing.

I decided to throw her a bone. I felt sure she wanted to know, so I asked Tony, "Who was that girl you were talking to?"

Peyton turned slightly. I knew her ears were alert as he answered, "Oh, she's one of my customers. She just had me install a stereo system in her boyfriend's car as a surprise for his birthday the other day."

"Oh, what a small world," I said.

Peyton's face relaxed. She was obviously pleased with his explanation.

In the last thirty minutes before the end of the meeting, they performed a play about God's presence here on earth.

In the play, a chubby young girl name Rose was cleaning her house. She prayed to God, asking him to visit her and have dinner with her. An angel of the Lord appeared to tell her that the Lord would visit her this afternoon. Very excited, Rose cooked a meal fit for a king and waited for Him. In the meantime, she had three visitors at three separate times, each asking her for some help. She hurried them away each time. At the end of the day, she got upset and complained to God that he did not keep his promise of coming to spend the afternoon with her. The angel reappeared to her and said, "The Lord did come. He first came as the beggar, then as your next-door neighbor, and then He tried one more time when He came as the parched, weary traveler."

Everyone in the room watched attentively, the atmosphere pensive and reflective. I identified with what Rose had done. I felt sure I'd asked God for things many times and He had sent them, but, because they weren't packaged the way I expected, I ignored them. I wondered what those things had been and I left determined to take a closer look at the gifts in my life. I no longer believed that they were coincidences. Everything happened according to God's purpose, orchestrated by Him.

Tony wanted to go as soon as church ended. It was 9:45 pm and his movie started at ten. Peyton had disappeared to the other side of the room, talking with a group of people. Tony said the he would wait outside; I should get Peyton and meet him at the car.

I scanned through the crowd, hoping to see Sean but no luck. They all stood in clusters, chatting and mingling with each other. The room sounded like swarms of bees had been let loose. I pushed through, smiling and responding to a few people who greeted me, all the while hurrying towards Peyton. I heard her saying goodbye to the group. I gave Eric a quick wave, then walked with Peyton towards the exit. We pushed through the double doors, the cool night's wind hitting my face so hard that I held my hair back.

"Whoa!" Peyton exclaimed, grabbing my hand to keep her balance. "What's this? It was not this windy when we got here."

We walked through the cars looking for Tony and then I saw him. Not only did I find Tony, but I found him, too.

"Oh, look who's here," teased Peyton. "Mr. On The Job Training. He's really getting cozy with the family. First your mom and now your brother; he is good."

"Oh, stop it," I said.

Sean stood next to Tony, deep in conversation.

When we came up to them, Tony held up his watch. "It's about time. The movie starts in five minutes."

Sean's eyes met mine, then Peyton's. He smiled. "Hello, ladies."

"Hi," I managed to say.

Peyton gave him a slight bump and said quietly, "You are good."

I wanted to kill Peyton, but I just stayed cool.

Sean's confused look was short-lived. He asked, "What movie are you guys going to see?"

Before Tony could answer, I said, "If you don't mind, I would like to go home. I'm really not in the mood for a movie."

Tony opened the car door and got in. Peyton whined. "Morgan, you said you would go."

"No, I didn't."

Tony grew agitated. "Well, at this point it's too late to take you home. The movie is about to start and we are still not there."

"Oh great," I said sarcastically.

Doomed, I prepared myself to spend the evening with these two and their misunderstood relationship.

As I opened the door, Peyton stuck her head out the window. "Sean, why don't you come along?"

He didn't take long to answer. "No, not tonight. Maybe another time."

I hadn't expected her to ask, yet his answer still disappointed me. Of course, he didn't want to go out with us—or maybe just me. It was Friday night; he must have somewhere to go or someone to see. I did my best to give him a genuine smile and said, "See you around, Sean."

I got in the car, then Sean said the most glorious words ever, "Morgan, if you want, I can give you a ride home."

Before I could respond, Tony said, "It's settled, then. Perfect! Morgan, get out."

"What?" I said, not sure what was happening.

Sean gave me his hand to help me out the car, that half-smile on his face. My knees grew weak. He must have felt it, because he held my hand tighter and rested his other hand behind my back.

"You okay?' he asked quietly as I nodded, suddenly embarrassed by my transparency.

I dreaded looking at Peyton, but could not avoid it when she got out the back seat to sit next to Tony. She had the biggest grin on her face as she passed us. She hugged me quickly, whispering, "I tell you…he is gooood."

Almost everyone was gone when I went back into Oasis with Sean.

"I'll be just a few minutes," he said.

I watched him as he hurriedly straightened the chairs and cleaned up the tables in the kitchen, filled with an assortment of soda cans and cups. I did my best to act as casual as possible. "Can I help you with something?" I asked.

"No, don't worry yourself. I'll be done in 2 minutes," he said pushing the cooler to the side of the kitchen,

I browsed the bulletin board, reading the various announcements and upcoming events: *Fish fry on October 30; Baptism November 16*, and a really interesting one — *Singles Ministry New Year's Ball and Gala*.

I moved on to the picture collage filled with shots from various projects in the community. I smiled at one of Mrs. Davis with a shovel, digging a hole for the Jamaica Housing Trust Dam Project, her face sweaty and tired. I couldn't help giggling when the next picture showed her laid in a stretcher and someone sprinkling her face with a bottle of water.

"What's so funny?" Sean asked as he stood beside me trying to decipher my amusement.

I forced myself to get serious; I didn't want him to know that I was laughing at his aunt. Then he saw that picture.

"That day was priceless," he said. "It was the first day that I moved in with Aunty. She decided to do this project with the Housing Trust. All the other ladies went inside the house to do less tiresome jobs, but no, not Aunty. She was outside with the men, trying to outdo them, when suddenly I saw my uncle running to her side. She was out cold. I still tease her about it all the time."

"I figured it was something like that."

We both laughed as we walked through the door.

Sean's car was the only one in the empty parking lot. I could see the road in the distance, filled with lights. Everyone was out on this Friday night. As we approached the road, the horns were blowing in succession, the normal sound of Jamaican living. The horn was as much a part of driving as the brakes. The smoke from the jerk pans filled the air and cars lined up, full of people waiting to be served. Sean turned the car around.

"There is way too much traffic. I'm going to take the back road through Norbrook."

"Oh, okay."

He turned onto the back street. I couldn't come up with anything to say, so we drove in silence. It didn't seem to bother him. I listened to the loud exhaust on his car until it started to to sputter, then got quieter. Then it stopped.

His car had slowed down a lot. Sean shifted desperately, moving his foot from gas to the clutch, but the car kept slowing down. The gears made an annoying screech before the car came to a complete stop.

"What is it?" I asked.

Exasperated, he rested his head back on the headrest. "Something that hasn't happened in a long time. I hate to even say it."

"What?" I insisted. "Are we out of gas or something?"

He turned to me with a humorous grin. "Right you are, Morgan, right you are."

He got out the car and I followed suit. "So, what now?"

"We need to find a gas station," he said, reaching in this trunk for a red gas container. "Left or right?"

"Um, which has a closer gas station?" I asked.

"They're about the same; I would say it is a twenty-minute walk either way. You think you can hang?"

Not really sure if I could, since I had worn my high black strappy sandal that I normally reserved for Peyton, but I heard myself saying, This way—let's go."

A bright green sign with glowing letters informed us that we walked on Birchwood Lane, a quiet street with only the sound of the wind ruffling the trees. We walked in the middle of the street lined with large, immaculate houses. From the road, I could see flickering lights and hear the faint sounds of dogs inside. Sean's car, growing smaller behind us, might have been the only car on the street all night.

Sean matched my slow, careful pace. The last thing I wanted to do was tumble over in my heels. He didn't seem to mind. Relaxed, he walked with one hand in his pocket and the other holding the gas can, kicking pebbles as he walked. I looked behind me, spotting his shadow. *Even his shadow is gorgeous*. I smiled at my pitiful thought and he picked up on my silliness.

"What's so funny?" he asked, breaking the silence.

"Oh nothing. I just remembered something Peyton said."

"What's that?" he asked naturally.

"It's nothing really," I said, looking away and hoping he couldn't see the lie in my face.

"So, Peyton," he said. "You guys are good friends."

"Best friends," I said. "She's my only friend actu-ally." *Not quite sure why I confessed that*.

"That's cool. You guys seem so completely different."

"How so?" I asked, though I knew how different Peyton and I were. I just wanted to get his take on it.

He cleared his throat as if buying time to figure out what exactly to say. "Well, not that I know much about either of you, but she seems very erratic and—I hope you don't mind me saying it—a little crazy."

I laughed at his description of Peyton. He was right on. I saw lights in the distance; it shouldn't be too far now. We stepped off the road for an upcoming vehicle, then continued in silence until I asked, "And me?"

He smiled. "I hoped you had forgotten. I'm horrible at describing people. I'm sure I offended you with my description of your friend."

"You are really not too bad—actually, right on."

"Okay, I feel a lot better now; I can say what I have to say with a clear conscience."

"Am I that bad?" I exclaimed.

"Well, that's for you to decide," he said evenly.

"Okay, let me have it."

"You, on the other hand, are a bit more reserved, purposeful and…"

He looked over at me and his piercing eyes sent shivers straight down to my feet. They became light and shaky. I faced forward, trying to stay composed.

He finally continued. "Not sure why, but I can't help thinking that you are scared of something."

I gave him one of his own slight smiles and kept walking. I couldn't say much to that. The truth was that he might be right. He didn't clarify his statement and, no matter how much I'd love to, I couldn't say, "I'm not scared of anything." So we didn't say anything else about it.

We both walked along, lost in our thoughts after his observations. The silence stretched on.

We kept going, enjoying the cool breeze and the usual sounds of the night. Sean started to kick all the stray pebbles on the road, like he was playing football with himself. I moved out of his way and up onto the sidewalk. My OCD kicked in and I made it a point not to step on the lines in the sidewalk.

Up ahead, the bright lights got closer. I could hear the faint blowing of horns. Sean snapped out of his meditation and must have seen my slight wobble because he asked, "How are your feet holding up?"

"Let's just say that I'm happy we are close."

He chuckled. Then an idea came to me. I remembered what Peyton said about the rumors she'd heard about him. I walked over next to him on the road and said, "Want to play a game?"

He looked at me curiously. "What game?"

"It's a game Peyton and I play from time to time. We haven't played in a while, but it was fun, from what I remember."

"Alright, let's hear it."

"So...the game is called Truth."

"Truth? Is it like truth or dare?"

"Um, kind of but not really. I guess the truth part is the same, but there is no dare."

"Okay, so how do you win?" he asked.

"You are such a guy, turning everything into a competition."

"Well, I'm just asking, since it's a game and all."

"So this is the game: we take turns asking questions and we have to tell the truth, no matter what. You win if the other person refuses to answer the question."

"What if no one loses?"

"Then we'll continue the game until someone does. Even if it is not today, the game continues."

"Alright, then," he said with a sigh. "Who starts?"

"I'll start so I can break you in," I said with a smile. "What's your favorite color?"

"Black," he answered quickly.

"Oh, so you're a shade lover, too; my favorite color is grey."

"Well, that is all dandy, but that was not my question."

We both laughed and I said, "Okay, let me have it."

He thought for a minute, then said, "I'll start off easy, too. When is your birthday?"

"December tenth, I'll be eighteen. When is your birthday?" I asked instinctively.

"April second."

"How old will you be?" I asked.

"I'll be twenty-one," he said."

"You'll be twenty-one, but you're already finished with college for almost two years now?"

"Yeah, I started at sixteen and graduated in three years."

"Wow, so we have an overachiever on our hands," I joked.

It took the loud car horns blowing, one after the other, to remind us that we had arrived at the gas station. We crossed the road and walked up to a broken yellow and red sign marked Shell.

"You okay?" Sean asked. By then, I was limping. I made my "I'm in the worst pain" look. He smiled.

"Let's do this. Come on, sit over here until I come back." He led me to a small table covered with black and white dominoes and two open beer bottles, situated in the corner of the gas station. I flinched and sat at the edge of one of the chairs. My feet were on fire and I felt blisters all over.

Sean ran over to the gas attendant, who began filling his red gas can. He walked to the side of the store for a minute and I couldn't see him. I got a little worried and stood up, but then I saw him coming back with a black plastic bag in his hand. He stopped to pick up his gas can from the attendant and headed towards me.

For his entire forty-second walk back to me, we kept our eyes fixed on each other. Staring in his eyes had become easier. Before, I used to feel flustered, but right here, for the first time, it felt right.

He handed me the bag that he was carrying.

"What is this?" I asked. I opened the bag to see a pair of yellow flip-flops.

"I really don't think you would have made it back," he said, grinning.

"I would have made it back quite fine," I lied.

Chapter 11

November

November third finally arrived, the day of Roxann's long-awaited Fall Fashion Show. I had dreamt of this day coming and going for the last three months and I longed for some peace and quiet; really, I just wanted some time to concentrate on myself and my needs. I woke up at five-thirty that morning, my head filled with thoughts of my final project for my Journalism 101 class.

I had been having a terrible dream about freezing in the middle of presenting my project. In the dream, while turning in the paper, I glanced at it to see that it had been blank! I couldn't remember anything, and I couldn't speak. When I woke up and realized it was just a dream, I felt extreme relief.

My classmates might have seen this as just another class in their college path, but not me. I had gone out on a limb to give journalism a shot, even though the wounds deep inside me screamed of hurt. Journalism raked up feelings of betrayal and lies. I wanted to stifle this dream, along with the others that, today, mean nothing. I wanted a sign about whether or not I should continue. This semester was really my journalism career interview.

I was interviewing it, and better yet, it was interviewing me.

My dad had always said, "Some things cannot be explained."

This holds true for a job or anything that interests a person. No one can explain why one person likes the color blue and someone else like red. It cannot be explained why one person is a diehard animal person and another isn't, or more specifically, why some are cat people, while others are dog lovers. Life doesn't always make sense; it just happens.

I suppose that's how my dad justified leaving his wife and two children behind. I could hear him now in my head, "It is what it is." My dad was an idealist, and not the good kind who has dreams and brings unique concepts into existence. He had dreams and got trapped in them, not realizing that he needed to wake up and face the life that he had been given.

I could almost understand why Roxann was the way she was. After dealing with my dad, she became very straightforward and practical. She didn't care much for dreams or dreamers. "Just do it," she'd say.

I wanted my final project to be relevant to life, not dreams. I wanted it to speak volumes to those who read it, but, first, I wanted it to speak volumes to me. I wanted a topic, a situation to write about, that lit a fire within me that would, in turn, infuse fervor and passion in my writings. I wanted to find my place and my calling; I needed to know beyond the shadow of a doubt that journalism was for me.

For Roxann, fashion design had always been her passion. She started sketching and making garments as a little girl. Peyton, who had always wanted to be a hair stylist, ate and breathed her skill. Tony loved cars so much that he made a career out of working with them. They all know who they are, have accepted it, and built their lives around it.

I felt like my passion formed an unseen part of my makeup. I was almost sure that journalism was the path for me. My challenge now was to make it seen. I have to prove to myself that I have found the right career for me. I considered this project my test and I was determined to pass. Prayer made me feel better. I honestly felt like my thoughts were being heard. Praying every day for the last two months, I had grown comfortable talking to God. I got down on my knees and spoke to Him openly.

Dear Lord, I need help. I cannot do this on my own. I mean, I will not try to do this on my own, because I will fail. Use me as a vessel and have Your way. Satisfy my concerns and show up like only You can. Make apparent my position. Take me off the fence and give me the surety that I need. Grandma always said that what the devil meant for evil, You will turn it for good. My dad has left and I don't know how to handle that, but You are still here. Help me with this project. Let it make the impact that I need to help in my healing. Thank You for always being here and answering prayers. Amen.

I got off my knees and something strange happened. A thought appeared in my mind—an inkling that had not been there before. I had a flashback to when Sean and I went to the debate. In an uncanny, inexplicable way, the feeling that surrounded me then rushed back.

I peeped into the backroom, chaotic with all the models getting ready for the show. The large, brightly lit room behind the stage was filled with a bunch of cackling girls and even a few guys. With showtime in twenty minutes, there was still so much to do. Peyton had three models sitting around waiting to get their hair finished. A couple of models had dropped out last minute, so Roxann had to alter their garments to fit their replacements. She crouched on the ground, pinning a long beige kimono dress onto her new model, who was a few inches shorter than her original pick. Lisa helped with makeup, while some of the girls crowded the mirror doing their own. Roxann shouted to them to make sure they did not get makeup on the garments. The five guys, all dressed, talked enthusiastically amongst themselves.

Before I could go back to my post, helping Aunty Madge collect payment and tickets at the entrance, Roxann called me over. I pushed through the crowded room in the long, grey chiffon couture dress that Roxann made for me. She gestured for her model to move on to the makeup station, then started working on the next model.

"How things going out there?" she asked.

"Great—most of the seats are filled and a few more people are still strolling in. Everything looks nice and the backdrops are ingenious."

"Alright, that's good. Tony finish setting up for the first scene yet?"

"Almost. He and Flex are finishing up now."

I left the room, heading back outside. I passed Tony and his friend Flex, behind the curtains with the backdrop structures, strategizing about when to change the set. They had two more backdrops to put up for the show and Roxann had two scenes each for her three backdrops. The backdrop for the first scene was a model of New Kingston with buildings the size of a person. The model, featuring the statues in Emancipation Park and the Pegasus hotel that I passed each day as I drove through New Kingston, looked so real. There were even small replicas of the concierges, decked out in their gray and red caps, opening the door to the little toy cars on the road.

Roxann called this scene *Coming to Jamaica*. The models would strut the stage in cultural garments like those of African and Oriental princesses. Roxann's inspiration for this scene came a few months ago when she saw an African family all adorned in their beautiful native clothes going into the Pegasus hotel in New Kingston. She said seeing them reminded her of the movie, *Coming to America*.

I pushed through the curtain, down the stairs on the side of the stage, and to the front to help Aunty Madge. The air outside was warm and the décor beautiful. Big lightbulbs strung around the trees of the courtyard and the easy tempo of Bob Marley created a relaxed atmosphere. *I want to love you and treat you right*, echoed through the speakers. The people, mostly well-dressed, chatted excitedly while waiting for the show to start. Nearly all one hundred and fifty chairs were filled. As I approached the entrance, a small line formed at the refreshment booth, where my Aunt Grace and Roxann's friend Marie sold refreshments. The openness of the night and beautiful ambiance made for a perfect stage for what should be a great show.

At the gate, Aunty Madge had everything under control. Two people filled out their raffle tickets and one more person waited to get in. The music stopped, then the rhythmic beating of drums started slowly. It sped up, then stopped suddenly. The curtains opened and the spotlight shone on the beautiful backdrop of New Kingston. The hotel model stood tall, each of the windows shone with lights, bringing the stage to life. The audience clapped, *oohed*, and *ahhed*.

Two models, dressed similarly in shimmery maroon wrap dresses walked onto the runway, dropping colorful rose petals. They quickly disappeared, clearing the stage for a stunning African princess dressed in a deep purple gown with a fluffy train that flew in the wind. The crowd gasped in delight. I smiled as the press in attendance scurried to take the pictures as the models came out. The reaction was the same for every model and every scene.

I walked backstage to see if I could get a glance of the beautiful mountain that Roxann and I saw when she fell in love with this venue during my orientation. I stepped into the small well-lit gazebo surrounded by plants and sat, peering through its nonexistent walls at the mountain's silhouette, still apparent even in the dark. I gazed, soaking up the lucidity from beholding God's beauty.

I turned quickly when I heard footsteps. I was stunned, but pleasantly so, when I saw that it was Sean.

"Hey, you," he said, stepping up to join me in the gazebo. He leaned on the pole at the entrance.

"Hey, I didn't know you were here."

"I'm here," he said, stretching his hands out. "Aunty begged for company. I saw you earlier, but you were running around."

"I know; this has been a crazy day. I think I'm high on hair spray."

"So that's what's holding your hair up," he joked.

"You look nice," I said, trying to downplay my true thoughts. He wore fitted black pants, with a green, blue, and black striped shirt. His look was so effortlessly him. The truth was, I thought he would look great in everything. He had a swag that made everything look good.

"Well, I don't think you need to hear it from me, since you are clearly the best dressed person here, and you should be on the runway," he said, oozing all his charm.

I smiled, blushed, and then turned in the direction of the dark mountain.

"What are you doing back here anyway?"

"I wanted to find out if I could still see the mountain."

He joined me on the bench and stared with me into the blackness. "It is beautiful out here. I actually took pictures at this very spot for my photography class a few years ago," he said.

"You did?"

He shook his head. "The easiest A I ever made."

"Oh, that has more to do with the mountains than it does with your skills," I teased.

"Maybe, but I sure do have a knack for knowing true beauty," he said, staring at me. His piercing eyes narrowed and I couldn't help feeling he had directed that comment to me. Not knowing what to do, I faced forward.

He chuckled.

We heard clapping from the other side. Sean steered the conversation to safer topics, acknowledged the applause and commenting that Roxann was very good at design. He finally sat down on the other side of the bench with his elbows on his knees and his hand on his chin. I looked away from him into the distance. We sat there quietly, both comfortable with the silence. Obviously, we both had a lot on our minds.

I started thinking about my father and all the things in our lives that he had chosen to miss. He would have been proud of Roxann for doing so well and Tony for the man he'd become. I wasn't sure what he would be proud of me for; I was the only one who had checked out.

Sean stood up and it shook me back into reality.

"So, I think it's my turn," he said.

"Your turn for what?" I asked.

"You know, that game we played the other night where you have to answer my questions."

"Oh, you mean Truth."

"Yes, that's it—Truth".

The other night, we had played Truth all the way back from the gas station to the gasless car. We took turns, asking only basic questions. Neither of us was brave enough to ask anything too personal. We asked about each other's favorite ice cream, movie, music, and books. I found out that he had a little sister named June and a weird habit of brushing his hair before bed. He found out that I had a weird habit of only drinking dark juices and sodas.

Tonight, the cool night and the sovereignty of the mountain brought a certain seriousness to our dispositions. I knew tonight's questions would not be the same lighthearted ones as before.

He said he would start off easy, but he did anything but.

"Alright let's see…," he said.

He looked up and said softly, "What makes you so sad?"

"Sad? I'm not sad—aren't I always nice?"

"You are. I might be wrong," he said, getting up. He jumped up on the ledge of the gazebo and swung his legs. "Something troubles you and I just wanted to know what it is."

"Even if that's so, what's it to you?" I asked him, a little too defensively.

"Nothing, really. It's actually none of my business," he said flatly.

I felt a sharp stick in my heart at his matter-of-fact response.

"In case you forget, I'm just playing a game, a game that you introduced and so clearly gave me the rules for. If you can't manage to answer, forfeit and declare me the winner," he said, jumping off the rail.

He stood at the entrance of the gazebo with his back turned to me. I wasn't sure that I had actually answered because I had never heard those words come out of my mouth before. Normally, I recite them like a creed in my mind.

"I'm sad that life is so unfair. I'm sad that people's decisions can affect me. Why do people lie without feeling an ounce of remorse for hurting the ones who believed them?"

He turned to face me, but I looked down on the floor, away from him, before continuing.

"In a nutshell, my dad left me, he left us all, with no explanation that makes sense. How could he look at his little girl and his little boy and say, 'I don't want you anymore.' How selfish to bring children into the world, but leave when it becomes inconvenient."

I began sobbing, uncontrollable sobbing. My body jolted, making my voice shaky as this weakness that I couldn't stop overtook me.

"Nothing in life makes sense to me anymore. So I do stare blankly, probably looking really sad, because nothing matters and everything is just a matter of time."

Sean looked concerned. I would bet he hadn't been expecting that when he started probing. I felt like a feeble little child crying in front of this cryptic stranger. I knew hardly anything about him, but I had poured out my fears and struggles to him.

"Morgan...I'm sorry that he did that."

His voice was soothing, empathetic and comforting. He sat next to me, obviously troubled by my confessions.

"You know, you're right. Life isn't fair. People are selfish and messed up in the head."

He spoke with such conviction and seriousness, his head bent, trying to get my attention. With my chin down to my chest, I bit my lips, trying to stop my tears.

He continued in the same soothing voice, like he wanted me to understand what he was saying.

"People do make decisions that adversely affect the people around them, without being concerned. I felt a lot like you do not so long ago in my life. I was angry at the system and the cruel people who surrounded me. I could not be convinced that people were good because I only saw worldly people, evil ones, with their own agendas. There was no one to trust, not even those who claimed to love me. I was sent here under less than great circumstances, angry with the world for all the bad cards that it dealt me. I'm still working on being the person I know I will become."

"What changed?" I asked.

"I made a conscious decision. One day I thought, how stupid to have other peoples' actions dictate the outcome of my life. After all, it's my life. I'm sure the purpose stamped on my life wasn't 'stay pissed off after people have wronged you.' It wasn't easy and it's still not at times, but I will my way to life each and every day."

I stared at him, passionate in his determination, the veins on the side of his head showing through his smooth skin. He was on a mission and no one could throw him off course. I admired his strength, courage, and desire to be elevated above his circumstances. And then I realized that I didn't know anything about his situation. I don't want to pry, but I genuinely wanted to know more about him. He appeared bothered by the thought of what he had to overcome. I decided to ask my Truth question.

"What brought you back to Kingston?" He glanced up at me, then looked away.

"How about we make this easier," he said. "Just tell me what you've heard and I will confirm or deny and fill in the blanks."

Another round of clapping sounded from the stage. I could hear Roxann thanking her many sponsors, models, and guests. That might explain my quick, insensitive summary of what I heard.

"Okay. I guess I don't have time to tell you the long list of offenses rumored about you," I joked. "But to sum it up, you are a hardened criminal—or better yet, you beat a police officer—and ended up in jail, but were sentenced to a lifetime of community service instead, thanks to your big shot lawyer father and his contacts."

He turned to face me with a weird look on his face. It wasn't the look that I'd grown used to. Recently, I'd only seen the nice Sean, always joking and laughing at me under his breath. Now he looked at me with a mixture of confusion, resignation, and a hint of annoyance. He didn't say anything, but quickly pulled himself together. He got to his feet and started walking slowly. He turned and said, with the slightest hint of disdain, "You have the story correct, Morgan; there's nothing to add or deny here. You have me down to a T. Happy we could get that out the way. You have a great night."

I heard the sound of his shoes in the wet grass, as he disregarded the walking path and headed straight for the cars. Before I could think of what to say, he disappeared past the stage.

I sat there for a few moments longer, staring back at the blackness of the mountain. My thoughts and my mind, running a mile a minute, were still not quick enough to make sense of what just happened.

Was I not supposed to tell him what I heard from Peyton? Did I offend him? Why was he mad? Does he think I believe the rumors? I was just relaying what I heard—I thought that's what he wanted.

I got up to find him and apologize. When I got to the other side of the stage, it was too late. The place was almost empty and he was nowhere in sight.

Sean

The first time

Sean didn't know for sure that she knew who he was, but that's fine. Actually he'd left not wanting her to think that he was weird. It was the day of his first meeting with the JLP garrison leader, Neily Ram and the PNP garrison leader, Scaggy Dunns. They stood on opposite sides of the street like statues posing for media. Both men faces stern, crossing their hands, while the people in orange and green walked by.

The street was crowded with media representatives from all over, ready to tell the nations of this new initiative to bring peace to the streets during this election. Sean walked with the people on the side blending in while wearing his orange and green shirt and red bandana. A style that Marsha in marketing suggested for the march that day and for the first few interviews Sean would have with both men in the coming weeks. He honestly felt ridiculous and would rather be wearing a white t-shirt. But that's neither here or there, they do things differently and he just went with it.

Back to earlier in the day, when Sean saw her for the first time. His aunt asked him to take her to the plaza to get a dress for an event she had that night. He left his aunt at the plaza and went by the bank. When he returned, he checked a couple of stores, trying to see where his aunt ended up. He was already in his orange and green shirt prepared for the rally. He walked into this store, Lee's. The store was filled with lots of chattering women.

He heard a girl say, "Good Afternoon, welcome to Lee's." Her voice was chirpy and youthful and after scanning the room quickly, he didn't see his aunt. Although, the girl was helping multiple people at a time, she was still looking at him and smiled as if he was the only one there. Sean was happy that he had his sunglasses on, remembering his odd attire that day. He quickly stepped back to leave, but not before taking a last glance at her. She seemed like she had something more to say, but he had already stepped out to continue looking for his aunt.

Sean didn't think more of it until that Friday night. He was bringing in cases of sodas into the church, this now being one of his jobs to satisfy his community service. They had just started singing and he walked quickly as usual avoiding any interactions. Just as he was going to open the door to the kitchen someone jumped in front of him helping him with the door. He glanced slightly and was a little surprised that it was her again. Him thinking that made it difficult to speak and before he knew it, he moved quickly through the door. He threw the soda down on the floor wondering why he was impacted by this person. It's like she renders him speechless.

After church is when it really got weird. Sean had a system - He handed the soda quickly to them as they left. He even tried putting a few at a time on the counter to avoid any unnecessary contact with anyone. He was just a man on a mission doing his time. He noticed that he ran out of the ones on top of the counter and turned to get a few more from the cooler. He felt someone walking up to the counter and while still in the cooler he shouted, "what flavor?" The person responded, "grape!"

"*Grape*?" he thought. He stood up and spun around to show his annoyance. It was her and just like that it happened again. He couldn't find the words to say. He just stared at her until she eventually turned away. He finally said, "we don't have grape." He tried to stay nonchalant saying it in the flattest way possible. When she asked for a coke instead, he turned and picked one from the cooler. He handed her the coke. She flinched a little and he noticed her flushed cheeks. She quickly turned to leave, and he couldn't help but to take one final look as she walked away.

Chapter 12

The next two weeks passed in a blur. I felt even more removed from the reality of life. Trapped thoughts clogged my head with no way to escape. I hadn't heard from Sean. I tried calling him after our misunderstanding the night of the fashion show, but only got a recording saying that his mailbox was full. After that, I let go of any crazy illusions I had about him. What was I thinking anyway? I knew better than to ever let anyone get close.

With my delusions out the way, I spent two days researching topics for my final project. Ms. Logan explained that our final project should be life changing and groundbreaking. She believed that all eighteen students could present a controversial story or idea with enough evidence to support a thesis statement. All the questions did not need to be answered, but we should present enough evidence to stir up emotions and evoke interest in our readers. The readers would be Ms. Logan and a committee of teachers, who would vote for the winning theory. That student would receive an automatic A in the class and the entire class would work on their winning story idea in our Journalism 102 class next semester.

Nothing spectacular came to my mind. Everyday societal interest topics like the inflated economy and horrible roads around the island left me bored. I was sitting at the small computer, downstairs where my dad used to sit, and about to climb back into my glum mood. Then it happened. The scripture "don't worry about anything; instead, pray about everything" came to mind. Although I didn't want to, I said a little prayer.

Oh Lord, I'm sorry for being in such a bad mood recently. I promise to talk to You more—after all, I have no one else. I'm sorry to only come to You when I need something. I will try to change that, too. Please Lord, help me to find a topic for my final project. Not just any topic, but one that was created for me to write and speak on. I thank You for answering prayers and I believe that I will receive an answer from You.

I opened my eyes and saw, almost as if it had been strategically placed, a yellow piece of paper sticking out of the cupboard at the bottom of the desk. I didn't know how long it had been there or why I felt the need to look at it. As I pulled on it, the door of the cupboard swung open and a stack of papers tumbled down on my hand. I still managed to hang on to the yellow sheet.

I opened the folded paper and read the notes on it, an invigorating feeling spreading through my body.

The extortion of the government continues with fixed elections. The winner has already been selected.

On the list was also a list of names, election terms and places.

Call back—Hurace Bucannan—

Interview Lance Hall-Minister of Election

Areas at risk for election rigging: Runstown, Trelawny, Bakersville, Mandeville, Charlesfield, St. Thomas—

Neily Ram—Jungle leader

DOE—Courtney Price

2 Term Election winner – 1st Term PNP, 2nd Term JLP

Call the Electoral Office

I held the paper for a moment wondering what it was. I recognized my father's handwriting. My father had been known for leaving random writings around the house, but I hadn't seen any of them in years. *Why did I find this paper at this precise time?* Overwhelmed with emotion and confusion, I grabbed the note and ran upstairs to my room. I closed the door and curled up on my window seat, thoughts flooding my head. My mind flashed back to the debate that Sean took me to a few months before. I remembered the electrifying awareness of corruption that pulsated through my body, the scent of extreme injustice.

I had told Sean about two teams playing a game with a crowd that already know who would win. At the time, I really couldn't put what I felt into sensible words, but now it seemed plain. My gut had been screaming that the election was fixed. What a coincidence that my dad had notes on this very topic! I wondered what he had found out, then a feeling of outrage took hold of me. The journalist in me came alive.

I heard myself say, "The people need to know."

The people need to know. This is, after all, a democratic society. *How can elections be fixed?* That would change the very history and integrity of our nation. I'm not a stickler about many things in life, but deception and outright injustice and corruption are unacceptable. People can do wrong because it's in their nature; it is impossible to have all good people. However, there has to be a group of people, in this case, the government, that holds people accountable to the standards that shape our society. It is intolerable that they exploit their power and hide behind the illusion that the people choose their leaders, while actually selecting one on their own.

I sat there, wondering what to do with this new discovery. One thing I knew for sure was that I had found the topic of my final paper.

I heard sounds downstairs. Roxann called my name, snapping me back to reality. One thing I knew for sure, I could not have her know about the note that I had found from my father. I folded it up and stuck it in my pocket.

I needed to talk to Sean. I felt like he could help me to make sense out of nonsense. I called him one more time using the house phone. I was surprised when he picked up. He played if off as if he wasn't surprised to hear my voice. I asked him if he could come over to my house, right now. After he spent too much time probing into why I needed him, I told him it was an emergency and I didn't have anyone else to call. My pitiful plea worked. He reluctantly agreed to come within the hour.

I ran into Roxann in the kitchen, unpacking groceries. I helped her, sparking small talk about the store. Once started, she happily went on and on about her business booming since the fashion show. I encouraged her preoccupation because, if she hadn't been talking, she might have picked up on my distraction. I tried to interject at the right moment, but the note I had just read filled my mind. As I put the last of the groceries in the refrigerator, her phone rang.

I used that as my cue to leave. I grabbed my folder and told her I was going on the patio to wait for Sean to help me with one of my assignments. She answered her phone and, as I left, I heard her telling my aunt about my delusions of journalistic grandeur. "That one Morgan stay just like her father. She has to figure out everything on her own. I tell her this journalism thing a waste a time, but she still wants to see for herself."

I went outside to meet Sean at the fountain, too anxious to wait on the patio. I wanted to make sure he didn't knock on the front door and ask Roxann about my emergency. I checked to see if I looked okay and was taken aback by my findings. I stood there in yoga pants and a tie-dye shirt that Roxann made during one of her fads with my hair in a messy ponytail and my feet swimming in Tony's flip-flops. I shrugged, then sat on the fountain's edge to wait for Sean.

I ran my fingers under the water until later the loud noise from Sean's car announced his arrival, preceding him by thirty seconds. He jumped out of his car and started towards me, in full black this time—black jeans, a fitted black t-shirt, and dark sunglasses. He stood in front of me pulled off his glasses, and asked, "So what is it?"

I felt a quiver down my spine. His striking presence never failed to affect me. I tried to look past his blunt introduction and disinterested glare. Obviously, what I said the other night still bothered him.

"Well, hello to you, too," I said sarcastically.

He continued staring, his icy glare matching his attire. Uncomfortable, I didn't know how to start. So I blurted it out. "So, I think I know the topic of my final paper."

He gave me a dumbfounded look, like the one he gave me when we first met and I asked for a grape soda—the *Are you serious?* look.

"You called me here to give me this news? This is the big emergency that took me clear across town, leaving me, at this very moment—" He checked his watch. "—two minutes late for an appointment?"

"Well, there is more, but we need to sit," I said.

He looked impatient, but he still followed me to the patio. From there, we could hear Roxann on the phone in the kitchen. I pulled out the yellow paper with my father's notes.

He glanced it over. "What is this?"

I explained my thoughts. My father had written these notes and I felt that there might be some truth to these allegations of fixed elections. "I want to write my final paper on this topic, but even more—if this is true, I want to get this story out. Everyone has a right to know and, if it's is true, it needs to stop."

He got to his feet. "If this is true, Morgan—and, I mean, that's a big 'if'—how do you plan on proving this? You're not a famous, respected journalist like your father."

"I was hoping that you could help me," I said softly.

He hadn't finished. "Better yet, how many people will you piss off by starting these rumors? Very ambitious, but you are in way over your head. Go back to the drawing board and find an easy topic that a first-year student can actually do in a month. Something that you can research in libraries and people will actually be willing to give you quotes for."

His tone was belittling and condescending and I didn't appreciate either.

I stood up, too, and told him angrily. "So is that how you decide what to write about? You chose the easy stories? What about what's right? It's really not about the paper for class; it's bigger than that. I thought that you would understand, but I guess not."

He put his sunglasses back on and said, "Sorry I couldn't be of more help, but we criminals don't always do what's right."

As he walked off, I was so infuriated that, when I looked down on my phone and saw his name in my contacts, I pressed delete. The same numb feeling swept over me as when he left me at the fashion show; when it passed, I felt a stab in my heart.

I had to get out of there; I didn't need Roxann asking why I was upset. I waited until he left, then got in my car. I really wasn't following him, but he hadn't gotten very far. I spotted his black, growling car a few spaces ahead of me.

The light turned green and he edged his way through traffic from the middle lane to the right lane. He turned onto the street and out of sight. By the time I got to the light, it turned red again. I looked down the street where his car turned and, to my surprise, there it was. He had parked his car on the side of the road, close to the streetlight.

After that, everything happened so fast. Someone got out of the car wearing a green shirt with orange writing. He wore the same glasses and bandana as the strange guy in Roxann's store a few months ago. Ordinarily, I would have left the situation alone, but the guy got out of Sean's car. The light turned green and I stalled for a moment, staring at the car, waiting for someone else—really, waiting for Sean to get out.

Overwhelmed and puzzled, I couldn't think how to react. Beeping assaulted my ears and loud voices shouted for me to get out the way, so I started through the light, then swung to the right and found myself parked behind his car.

My heart raced. *What am I doing here? Why does Sean have these kinds of people in his car? Why didn't he want me to write about the possible corruption?* I had too many questions and I wanted some answers. I said a little prayer asking God to protect me as I stepped out the car.

I walked over to the metal door that blended in with the corrugated metal fence, topped by barbed wires. The whole thing had been painted with a mural of a rose garden and, if I hadn't seen the guy just go in, I would not have known it was an entrance. The heavy door was hot to my touch. I pushed it cautiously, not knowing what to expect. It squeaked loudly as I slipped through.

It opened into a little courtyard with the sky as its roof. No one was in sight. I suddenly remembered how I was dressed, still in my yoga pants and Roxann-inspired tie-dye shirt. I stepped over a puddle of water and found a steep staircase wrapped around a corner, leading down.

I could hear buzzing below. I started down the steps, holding the wall and trying to not make any sounds. The sky disappeared; the dark staircase kept going, deeper into the ground. My pounding heart moved up to my throat. *Am I crazy?* My legs kept moving down into the ground. The sound below, though muffled, grew louder.

Why am I following that boy? Why do I have to know more? Why can't I be satisfied with what he tells me?

I stopped and took a deep breath. I needed to calm my racing heart. I decided to pray.

Dear God, please, please, please be with my right now. If this is something I'm supposed to be doing, please give me the will to continue. If not, please give me the strength to turn around and get out of here safely.

I opened my eyes, still not sure what to do. I didn't know what His answer to me was. I did know that I had come too far; there was no way that I could turn back now.

With my OCD fully charged, I counted the steps—
seventeen— that brought me to level ground. The noise,
almost like a market mixed with talking, laughing, and
music, sounded closer. I headed down a dimly lit hall.
I noticed several big holes along the wall. They looked
like small cellars or those below ground entrances
to basement apartments. In any case, they were big
enough to hide me, if needed. I kept very close to the
walls, planning to duck into one if I saw anyone coming.

I could taste my heartbeat now, but my adrenaline
had kicked in. I felt alive. I walked quietly. Lights came
up ahead on my left, then loud banging sounds and
shouts from a group of people. I froze, not knowing
what to expect. I spotted another pocket by the wall near
the lighted area. I decided I could take the seven steps
to hide myself, then see what was happening. Thankful
for flip-flops, I stealthily and swiftly made my way to
my hiding place.

I crouched down, leaning at an angle to see the
source of all the excitement. A large group of people,
mostly men, sat around a table playing a game. With
the loud banging on the table and the taunting gestures,
I knew it had to be dominoes. The thick crowd around
them held money in their hands as they cheered.

A fuzzy television played on the wall, the sound
swallowed up by the dancehall music blaring through
the speakers. It was almost impossible to breathe. A
few people smoked marijuana and drank liquor at a

bar counter. The girls dressed scantily; the men looked rough and unkempt.

What is Sean doing here? Why was a stranger getting out of his car? This is so far out of my comfort zone!

I had told Sean about the rumors of his criminal past, but he hadn't given me a chance to explain that I didn't believe any of them. Now I wasn't sure anymore.

I decided to get out of this hoodlum-infested den that I had stumbled into. Then something caught my eye. To my right, at the other end of the hall, three men stood talking. They look unrelated to the bar scene inside. One wore a suit, another had on regular clothes, and the third was that guy again, the one in the orange and green shirt. There was still no sign of Sean.

As soon as the men walked out of sight, I snuck out of my hiding place. I made it undetected as the game of dominoes got exciting. I started off the other way down the echoing hallway. *Why am I not turning around?*

The carved out stone walls must have been there for years. I wondered how this underground establishment came about. I felt sure that it had not been built for its current use. The farther I ventured down the long hallway, the darker and more ominous things got.

Random sounds echoed in the hall; I hugged the walls and moved watchfully. I saw something up ahead. Before I could tell what I was seeing, I heard voices behind me. I found a wall pocket just in time. I snuck in, closed my eyes, and held my chest, trying to keep my pounding heart in place. After a quick deep-breathing session, I was calm enough to look.

To my right, I saw what appeared to be cells. I couldn't count them all, but they seem to run to the end of the hallway. At least five, I guessed, five real cells with iron bars. I would have figured they were historical and probably thought nothing of it, except that I could hear sounds coming from one of the cells. Irregular sounds like someone tapping something quickly and randomly. More nervous than ever, I decided to find my way out of there as quickly as possible.

To my left, in the middle of the hallway stood the three men again.

I heard the man in the suit explaining why he had a problem with a thought process. My nervousness turned into disbelief as I heard his voice. I didn't believe it at first, but then I heard his name.

The man in the suit said, "I have to run. Sorry we couldn't talk more."

The other man said, "No problem, let's meet tomorrow, same time."

As they shook hands, one of them said, "Tomorrow then, Sean."

"Yeah, man. Tomorrow we'll have more time to get the story together."

Sean's voice came from the person dressed like a hoodlum in orange and green! More perplexed than ever, I knew that I needed to get out.

The man in the suit left quickly, but Sean and the other man conversed quietly for another minute. They bumped fists, then the man went back down the side corridor. Sean put his notepad in his bag and walked towards the exit. I didn't know much, but I knew it was time to go. Curiosity killed the cat and I couldn't help thinking I was the cat in this situation.

I slipped out of my hiding place and walked as quickly as I could without calling attention to myself. The side corridor where the man had gone was empty now. I quickly crossed it, heading for the exit and staying as close as possible to the wall. I passed the gathering of yelling people with blaring music. I glanced at them as I passed by; this time, two sets of eyes rested on me.

The bartender noticed me, but then turned away to pour drinks. The other was a girl smoking by the entrance of the wannabe club, wearing the shortest shiny leather shorts that I had ever seen. Even Peyton would not have been caught dead in them. This girl wore them with a yellow bra top that didn't give her breasts any sort of support. She narrowed her eyes at me as she blew out the smoke. I kept walking, trying to act like I belonged. She never said anything.

I got to the stairs. I walked up the first few to make sure I was out of sight, then ran as fast as I could out of the darkness. When I made it to the bright sunlight, I smiled and held my head up to the sun, ready to exhale and thank God for taking me out safely. Then I heard someone yell, "How you get in here?"

I shaded my eyes with my hand to see who spoke. A big black man sat on a chair by the entrance in a black shirt with the word Security on it. He stood up, his look demanding an answer. Something told me that I would need a really good reason to get by him.

Lord, please help me.

As cool as if I told the truth, I put out my hand and said, "Oh, you weren't here when we came in. I'm Tameka Porter; I came with Sean. I went to grab a drink at the bar and he left without me."

I sounded convincing and I hoped he bought it, because it was all I had.

"Oh, okay. You with Sean. He just leave about two minutes ago."

He believed me! And who would have thought it? The seven-foot gorilla can smile. I kept cool. "Yeah, he must be outside, waiting for me."

"So I'll see you tomorrow then, Tameka?"

"Maybe, we'll see."

He pulled the noisy gate open for me to get out. I stepped onto the sidewalk and looked back at the fence. The entrance disappeared into the picture of the rose garden again, but there was nothing rosy about that place.

The whole thing gave me the creeps. I walked down the road to where I parked my car. Sean's car was gone and, although the street was busy with cars honking, I didn't hear anything. I wondered what really went on behind that fence. I would never have dreamed that such underground operation existed. *Why would anyone, especially Sean, ever go down there?*

Then I remembered Roxann saying, "This is no country for young fools." I agreed more every day.

Chapter 13

spent most of the night awake. Thoughts flooded my head until I couldn't sleep. Disappointment kicked in and, although I tried to deny it to myself, there was no point. I was disappointed about Sean.

I wanted to get to know him, but the more I uncovered, the less I knew. I needed to talk to him, but what would I say? "I followed you into a dungeon and I need you to come clean about who you are." *How stupid!*

I knew absolutely nothing about this guy, except that the chemicals in my being reacted to the ones in his. I felt really sorry for myself. I could never say that out loud. I mean, I was silly about the whole thing; I was disappointed in a person who had never declared his feelings for me. I wasn't sure why this upset me; it wasn't like he committed a crime or anything. All the evidence added up to him visiting an unscrupulous place wearing a shirt with the colors of both parties. *What does that even mean? Why did he have to change clothes to go in that place?*

My heart tugged; I had a queasy feeling in the pit of my stomach. Morning couldn't come fast enough. I would doze off for fifteen minutes, then wake from at least one nightmare. In one of them, Sean found me underground and locked me a cell. In another, Roxann caught me out in public dressed the way I had been yesterday. The nightmares kept coming, so, after startling awake a few times, I gave up on sleep.

I stared at the ceiling, all my thoughts circling in my head. Finally, the night was behind me; the sun peered through my window, asking for my attention. I plugged my phone in to charge and saw a text from Peyton the night before, asking me to come with her to Oasis tonight. I had not been there in a few weeks; I hadn't even seen Peyton, I had been so busy with school. I texted her back.

Sure.

I wanted to make the best of today, since I had no classes on Fridays. I picked up my father's list from my desk and read it. I wondered where he got the notion that the elections were fixed. I needed to find out. I had less than a month before my final paper was due and I wanted to make it count.

After taking a quick shower, I went in my closet to find something professional for my adventure today. I bypassed the suits since I did not want to be too stuffy. I picked out a white pencil skirt with a short-sleeved fuschia silk top. I brushed my hair up in a ponytail and wrapped it to create a bun. I spent at least thirty minutes doing my makeup. When I finished, I hardly recognized myself. But I was on official business today; I needed to look like an adult to be taken seriously.

By the time I came downstairs, Roxann was already in the kitchen making coffee.

"Oh, I didn't know you were up," she said. "And look at you."

I smiled, knowing how happy Roxann got whenever I dressed up, especially in her creations.

"And you did your hair with the part on the side, just the way I like it."

"Yeah, yeah," I said wearily, trying to not make it a big deal.

The truth was that I had never paid this much attention to putting makeup on my face. I glanced in the mirror again, wondering who that person was.

"So where are you off to?"

"Oh, all over. I'm still working on my final project and have a few interviews."

"What are you working on and who you interviewing?"

I didn't know what to tell her. I could never tell her I'm attempting to investigate possibly rigged elections or where I got that crazy notion.

"I'm not sure yet. After my research, I'll know more. I'll tell you more maybe later."

She narrowed her eyes suspiciously. Surprisingly, she didn't press, but just took her coffee to the living room. I grabbed a banana and went to my car before she came up with another line of questioning. I pulled up to the electoral office thirty minutes later.

As I got out of the car, the people in the parking lot stared, making me feel uncomfortable. The office shared the plaza with Hilo Supermarket and a few small clothing stores that had their clothes hanging on racks outside. A line of taxi cabs filled most of the parking lot and the heat was ungodly. I needed to get inside before my heavy makeup decided to drip all over my silk blouse.

As I stepped on the sidewalk, I looked up to the second floor of the plaza. A big flashy sign there read *Urban News*.

Oh, that's where it is.

I quickly glanced at the parking lot behind me to check for Sean's car. I didn't see it, but I didn't see much of anything with the chaos from all the taxis.

The air conditioning inside the electoral office felt great. It was quiet in the office; no one even acknowledged that I had just walked in. There were seven desks, empty except for two people working behind the glass station. The two women looked down, busy working and I wondered which of them to approach.

Just then a young man came out to the back, dressed casually in jeans and a green sweater. He glanced at me, then did a double take. He smiled pleasantly and asked how he could help me. His nametag read Kevin. I walked over to him and introduced myself.

"Hi, I'm Morgan. I'm a student at UWI and I'm writing a paper on the voting process. I'm hoping to get a better understanding of this and all the various processes involved."

He seemed very interested, but he hesitated a bit. "All the information on how to register to vote is on the internet or you can follow these instructions." He handed me a yellow pamphlet.

This was not the information that I hoped to get. "I was hoping to spend some time here, observing the various procedures and operations."

"Well, I would love to help you but I'm just an intern here. I really can't make that decision. You may need to speak with O'Neil Baker, the operations manager."

"Oh, sure. Do you know if he's available?"

"Give me a minute; I'll check."

The women who ignored me earlier were now awake. The older of the two stared at me. I did my best to act normal and smile, but the best I could do was simper.

While I waited, I read the charts on the wall about every citizen's right to vote. Another one had the election theme written boldly in red, 'Every Vote Counts!'

Then a tall man in a black pants and white shirt came to the front with the intern.

"Yes, what can I do for you?" he asked in a friendly enough voice.

"Hi, I'm Morgan. I was telling Kevin that I have a final paper to write for one of my classes. I want to get a better understanding of voting process."

His stern face matched his demanding tone. "What's your angle? I mean, what's your thesis statement?"

"You mean, what's my take on this topic, right?"

"Yeah, what exactly are you wanting to prove about the process?" he asked.

The women, even more alert now, paid keen attention to our conversation. I stalled a little, definitely not wanting to tell the operations manager that I thought the process was flawed and the election fixed.

He sounded like a typical self-righteous uptown man as he continued. "Young lady, it's been a while since I've been out of school, but I do remember that you need a purpose statement; one that you are trying to validate. So, what is it?"

I was nervous and not prepared for this, but I didn't want him to know that. With no time for a long prayer, I prayed inside, *Lord, help me*. Just then my eyes were directed to the red writing on the poster in the office.

"Well, this is my first year at the University and my first year to vote—that's if I make the registration deadline, which is a few days after my birthday in about two weeks. We have to share our topics and papers with our classmates. With the election on its way, I really wanted to choose a topic that is relevant now. I don't know the procedures in place to prove that statement—" I pointed to the red words on the poster. "—but I would love to know. So I guess my purpose statement, and what I want to validate, is, does every vote really count?"

He looked at me, almost amused, and said, "Of course every vote counts." He started to gesture behind him at all of the state of the art equipment that they had.

I stopped him. "That is exactly the information that I need to gather to assure a bunch of new age college students who don't yet know the importance of voting that their votes will, indeed, count."

And, just like that, I got into the electoral office. Mr. Baker gave me permission to come into the office in the afternoons to observe and gather information to answer the question for my paper. He even suggested Kevin act as a mentor while I was there. Kevin, also a UWI student, was studying political science and doing this internship as a program requirement.

I spent most of the afternoon with Kevin while he explained the processes to me. He mentioned that every parish on the island had districts or constituencies and voting stations. He explained how there were no more ballot boxes. Instead, every polling station would have new electronic voting machines. The votes from the machines would all be sent to one master, state-of-the-art counting machine housed at their location in Kingston. That machine would tally all the votes from all the stations. Kevin was enthused and proud of the system, while I thought of questions about each of the processes.

I went home that evening and wrote down all my questions. *How do they select workers in each parish? Who makes sure the workers do the right thing? How state-of-the-art are these machines? Where are the machines kept?* I had a bad feeling about it all and I couldn't wait to go back next week.

That evening Peyton came over so we could go to Oasis together. I did my best to fill her in on all the latest happenings, something I don't usually do because I normally have nothing to say. She looked at me intensely, but listened quietly, as if she never heard me speak before. I could tell she did not know what to say.

She walked in my closet a few times, pretending to look for clothes, but I knew the conversation was unchartered territory for her. Usually, I listen to all her exciting drama. I needed to get some stuff off my chest, but it felt weird to talk so much. A few times I almost just wrapped up the story, but I kept going. I told her about the note with my dad's handwriting, about calling Sean for help, and his reluctance.

"Why is he not talking to you?" she asked.

I told her about the other night at Roxann's fashion show.

She rolled her eyes. "Men. Is it that serious?"

I hesitated a little before telling her about the scene from the movie, which was how I'd started thinking of it. Only in a movie starring me would I have been underground following a guy. I told her how I found myself at an underground bar or club or maybe even a jail after following Sean. Her eyes widened when I mentioned having to hide. I told her that Sean was the strange guy who scared me a few months ago at Roxann's store. As we pulled into Oasis, I told her about the run-in with the security guard at the exit. Peyton didn't say anything, but I could tell that her mind was going a hundred miles a minute.

"What?" I asked.

"You don't want to hear what I have to say right now. Let's just go into church. You will hear what I think later, though," she said with a smirk. "Quick question— you said that he was supposed to meet the men again today. Did you go back?"

"No, I thought about it, but I was stuck at the electoral office. Plus, I was scared."

She laughed at my pitiful confession. "Actually, that is a good thing."

We arrived just before the start, while other people were still walking in. My hair was still in an updo from this morning and I wore a fitted, burnt orange dress that fell just below my knees. Peyton looked bright and colorful in her short, lime green and blue polka dot baby doll dress.

The lights were already dim and the disco ball rotated around the room. The room was almost full, but we found seats to the side, where we always seemed to sit. Peyton's polka dots glowed, making me laugh.

"What?" asked Peyton.

I tried to stop laughing, but it was no use. She looked like a part of the room's décor. Between her and the disco ball, it was all too much for me to stay composed.

Peyton looked down at her dress and caught on. "Cool! I'm glowing, Morgan."

Her pleased comment made it even funnier. I kept laughing until the praise team began to sing. Two guys and three girls took the stage, all looking like they were a part of an army. They moved their bodies from side to side, singing.

> *I am a warrior, a warrior, a warrior, a conqueror*
> *I am a child of God and I've got victory*
> *Don't speak defeat, don't speak defeat to me*
> *I am a child of God and I've got victory*
> *I am a warrior, a warrior, a warrior, a conqueror*

All the young people in the room jumped to their feet dancing along with the singers on the stage. Peyton jumped to her feet and joined the parade. Redbone Eric moved toward us and Peyton met him halfway. They hugged and danced alongside each other. I watched, in awe of their energy. The whole moment felt like a combination of a flash mob and zumba class.

I felt someone watching me and, sure enough, there he was, leaning on a pole in front of the kitchen. I glanced at him, then looked away quickly. When I turned in his direction again, his eyes were still fixed on me. I managed to give him an uncomfortable smile. To my surprise, he smiled back.

I turned back to Peyton, who now had an entire circle of people around her. Jumping and dancing, she signaled for me to come over. I laughed and shook my head. Then she started twitching and bopping her head in Sean's direction. I smiled, pretending to not understand.

All the same, I was about to steal another look at him, but, as I turned, my eyes locked on his. He stood right next to me.

"Oh, I'm sorry. I didn't see you coming over." I said nervously.

He sat down next to me, looking simple yet sublime in a short-sleeved white button up shirt with dark blue jeans. My heart melted all over again. I was truly annoyed with myself and I guess it showed on my face.

"What's wrong?" he asked in his soothing voice, the one that I had grown used to before his stiff, angry voice surfaced.

"Nothing," I managed to say. I felt so uncomfortable that I just faced forward, looking at everyone worshipping. They had their hands raised and singing,

Here I am to worship
Here I am to bow down,
Here I am say
That You're my God
You're altogether lovely
Altogether worthy,
Altogether wonderful to me

Sean sat in his usual position with his fingers entwined. I couldn't think of anything to say or do. I couldn't concentrate on worship with him next to me, especially in light of our recent falling out. I closed my eyes, trying to block everything out and center my thoughts. That was when he started talking. I opened my eyes, but did not look his way.

"I want to apologize for the other night at the show," he said slowly.

I turned to him with a very soft look, but still didn't say anything.

He continued. "You were upset and I was not sensitive to that, but what can I say? It's the downfall of being a man. I mean, it was really unfair for me to take offense over something that you heard. I'm just tired of people putting in their two cents without knowing the truth."

He seemed sincere and really bothered by the gossip.

"Just to be clear," I said. "I didn't take one word of anything I heard seriously." Even though, in light of recent underground events, I wasn't so sure of this anymore.

"Why don't you believe what you heard?"

I thought about the question. *Why don't I believe what I heard about him?* I searched high and low for an answer, but nothing came. I said, pathetically, "I don't know why; I just don't."

He didn't say anything, but his demeanor said it all. He looked pleased and happy that I felt that way.

Peyton came by, interrupting our moment. "Ahem."
We smiled and she continued her worship.

Sean excused himself. He had to set up refreshments in the back. I listened to two young people, a really tall guy with a bright orange shirt and a heavy-set girl in a plaid dress, speak on the importance of being the person God made you to be. The girl spoke about following your own heart and your own dreams. She said that we could not follow anyone else's dream because we were not made for other people's tasks, but we were made and equipped for our own calling.

It made me think. Everything they said related to unleashing the gifts and powers that are already inside us. They even said that, while we are busy waiting for God to grant us desires and answers, we already possess them. We often hold ourselves back, refusing to birth what He's placed in us. Comparing it to birth suggested that it would take hard work to get our gifts from the inside out. Almost like a woman in labor who gets a beautiful child, but not easily. She had to carry the gift for nine months and, after that, you would think that her gift should just be handed to her since she did so much already. Yet she still has to push, sometimes for a long time, to birth her blessing.

I wondered what all my gifts might be and if I was willing to do what it would take to birth them. I left church that night contemplating a lot in my mind, including one big question. *Am I ready to show up in my life?*

That night, I laid in bed, watching the glare of the lights that snuck through my blinds. My head felt like a jigsaw puzzle. I had so many things to work on and no solutions for any of them. I was writing a paper about fraud in the electoral process. I was about to embark on a three-week venture of visiting the electoral office each week in hopes of finding clues to back that up. I was trespassing in an underground establishment, following someone who, for all I knew, was a criminal. *I must be losing my mind!* The first sign of insanity may just be doing things contrary to your normal self. *I am the responsible one. How did I become a hazard to myself?*

I closed my eyes, but it was no use; the pieces of the jigsaw puzzle began to spin. Clearly I needed a midnight snack.

Two big scoops of chocolate ice cream later, I lay on the plush woven couch in the living room. Roxann was sleeping and the house was quiet. The lights from outside glared through the window. I felt like a zombie, just staring into the darkness. I heard a car outside and figured it was Tony. I was tempted to find the remote to turn on the television, but I was too dazed, so I just stayed in the dark, motionless. I heard the shaking of his keys, then the door rattled and swung open. Tony came in the living room and turned on the light, jumping a little when he saw me in the couch.

"What you doing down here in the dark?" he asked, clearly spooked.

I chuckled a little. "Nothing. Can't sleep."

He sat down on the other couch and turned the TV on. He focused in on the TV, reminding me of how much he resembled my father. They both were tall with a muscular build, but it's the way he focused on the TV that reminded me most of my dad.

My father would always focus deeply on anything that he did, almost like going into a trance. Tony did the same thing as he scrolled through the channels. Something so effortless should take no thought, but they met it with such concentration. A thought came to me. Maybe it wasn't so much that they concentrated on what they were doing, but that they used trivial actions as a distraction from their real thoughts.

Without hesitation, I asked him, "What's wrong?"

"Huh? What's wrong with what?" he asked, seeming startled out of his thoughts.

"You seem distracted," I said. "Just making sure that you're okay."

"I'm good," he said nonchalantly.

I decided to ask small questions to see if he would open up. "So, where are you coming from at 2:40 am?" I asked lightheartedly.

"Movies," he said flatly.

"A movie this late?"

"And some food after that," he added.

"Oh, I see. Who did you go with?"

"I don't need nobody to go with."

"So, you went to the movies by yourself?"

"Yeah, what's wrong with that?"

"Sad, if you ask me."

"Well, I went by myself, but I did see your friend when it was over."

"What friend? I only have one friend."

"Exactly. I saw Peyton when it was over."

I wasn't sure what he was getting at. "Yeah, she left with Eric and some other people after church," I said.

He went on to say that she asked him for a ride home and they were both hungry, so they stopped at Cudgis to eat.

I wondered if that had anything to do with him seeming preoccupied, but I just acted casual. "Oh, okay."

I couldn't let it go, though. "So she left Eric and asked you to drop her home?"

He didn't answer, but he did ask, "So is he her boyfriend?"

"I think so, or close enough."

"Seem like a good guy," he said.

"I guess. I still feel like she could do better, though. I know this really great guy that likes her and I think she likes him, too."

"Yeah, which guy?" he asked.

"You don't know him. It's just someone at my school that she met when she came to visit me one day."

"How do you know that she likes him? Did she say that?"

"No, she didn't say it; neither did he. I just see the chemistry."

He made a little grunt of acknowledgement, but he didn't say anything more. He kept flipping through the channels then sank back into the couch. I didn't ask anything else. I left him alone with his thoughts and walked up to my room.

The weekend had its low points, but it also had its highs. I started off by reflecting on the funk that I had been in, then decided that I hadn't been in a funk at all. I just needed to be a doer and not a thinker. Thinking led me to feel defeated, so I decided to do my part in getting the outcome that I wanted. I prayed and ask God to give me strength.

I also thanked God for my mom, for Tony, for Peyton, even for Sean. I thanked Him for the blessings and the opportunities that He had placed in my life. I thanked Him for my professors and for the things I learned each day. I thanked Him for victories like coming out of an underground establishment alive and for getting the opportunity to shadow at the electoral office. I promised Him that I would do my part to succeed and I knew that He would help me where I fall short.

Chapter 14

December

Monday morning, I got up determined and focused. It was December 5th and I had seventeen days before my final project was due. I went to school, but I couldn't wait for it to be over so I could go by the electoral office. At exactly twelve-thirty, I pulled up to the office.

Today I wore all black, which, oddly enough, helped me appear focused as I stepped in confidently. I didn't slow down to be extra nice to the rude women at the front. As I walked behind the counter to find Kevin, I gave them a pleasant enough, "Good afternoon."

On my way to his cubicle, I met Kevin coming out of the auditorium. As he closed the door, I could hear the muted sound of chatter and claps.

"Hey, you, what's going on in there?" I asked quietly.

As always, Kevin had dressed nicely in grey slacks, a white shirt, and a red tie. He looked pleasantly surprised to see me, then looked me up and down.

"Oh, just a community meeting," he replied.

"What's it about?" I asked

"It's a meeting with Trident, the company that made the software for the new voting machines," he explained.

As I walked with him back to his desk, he continued, "They are here to show some members of the community the benefits of using this kind of program to count votes."

He picked up a folder from his desk, then we started back in the direction of the meeting. As we walked, he said, "We've been working on this community event ever since I started—actually, it was my idea. I was surprised Mr. Baker agreed to it, but he wanted to find some ways to engage the small business owners and the middle-class members of the community to come out and vote."

"Is it open to the public or is it invitation only?" I asked.

"We targeted households in specific areas within a median salary range and left out any extremes. That group of people is not big on voting. They feel that the system is corrupt and only benefits the very poor or the super-rich. One group benefits from the bribery and the other group facilitates it. That left the middle class stuck somewhere in the middle, feeling that their votes don't even matter," he explained.

"So, what is Trident doing here?" I asked.

"Well, the electoral office wanted to move away from hand counting ballots, which have proven problematic over the years. Trident is demonstrating how this new machine and program will do away with any unfair and illegal voting practices. We hope that giving these groups assurance that their votes will be counted will bring back credibility to the voting process," he said.

He swung open the auditorium door, signaling for me to go in. He walked in behind me and we took seats at the back. The room, a good size, had a red sign on the wall indicating a 300-count capacity, although it wasn't even quarter full. I could see about ten tables with eight or so people at each.

I whispered to Kevin, "How did they get so many working people here in the middle of the day?"

He pointed to the table at the side, where two women and a man dressed in uniforms stood loading plates onto trays.

"Free lunch," he answered.

The man at the front, a skinny tall man with glasses, directed a pointer at the screen, demonstrating the machine's features. "The machines will be in secure locations within the various districts. Votes will be recorded in real time and the person or party that you vote for will be confidential. There is only one screen in the entire country that will show and tally the votes as they come in. That one master piece of equipment will be housed right here at the electoral office," he assured them.

There was some pleased chattering.

"Wow, that is really good," I said to Kevin.

He smiled.

I took out a pen and paper to start taking notes. Just then, a waiter came over and brought us lunches, too. We almost explained that we weren't really a part of the group, but when we saw the crispy golden-brown fried chicken on top of the flaky rice and peas, we quickly reached out and took it.

The demonstration finished a few minutes after we finished eating. Back at Kevin's desk, I asked him the list of questions that I had written down a few days earlier. I asked him about the various locations throughout the country where the new voting machines would be housed. He looked at me skeptically and asked why I needed that information for my paper.

"I just want to give a detailed account of the process. I don't want to leave any stones unturned and I want them to know that this is really an official operation."

"Fair enough," he said, pulling out a map. There are five locations in each parish." Then he started going over the different names at random. At first, I didn't notice anything about the names, but then he offered this additional information.

"You know something interesting that I learned the other day?" Kevin, a nerd who lives for the world of politics, came alive.

"What is it?" I asked eagerly.

"There are a few locations where everyone knows who will win."

"There are?" I asked, very interested.

"Yeah, they've been voting the same way for the longest time. That's why you see different areas wearing one party's colors; it is basically their territory. For instance—" On the map, he pointed to the location in Tivoli Gardens. "JLP will most definitely clinch the vote in that location. The powers that be have already established themselves in that area."

I knew what he meant by 'established.' That was what Roxann complained about; people who got free electricity and water and were unwilling to work, but willing to vote for the party that benefited them.

"So, what's the point of an election if you basically already know what will happen?" I asked.

"Well, not every location is so predictable; there are locations, especially the ones with a large middle-class population, where it could go either way. Certain groups of people generally listen to the facts and make well-informed decisions without the agenda of the rich or poor. Both candidates go to many impromptu town meetings in these areas, trying to appeal to the working people. They take a different approach than they generally take with the other groups. People in the middle or working class want to know that the candidate has integrity and will do right not just by them, but by all. They listen to the views and values of the candidates before they decide to vote for them."

He pointed to two locations in working class areas that voted based on the viewpoints of each candidate, not just for a party. "For example—" On the map, he circled Runstown, Trelawny, Bakersville, Mandeville and Charlesfield, St. Thomas. "In the last two elections, spanning about ten years, the outcome from those locations determined who won the election."

The names kept screaming at me like an alarm or a fire drill in progress. Although Kevin kept talking, I didn't hear another word. I only wanted to look in my purse at the note that my dad wrote to see if the locations were the same.

At exactly 4:00 pm I left the electoral office and walked quickly to my car. The car seat burned hot from the afternoon rays; I cranked the air conditioning on high. Before leaving, I opened the folder with the map and the locations Kevin had circled. I searched in my bag for the paper with my dad's scribbled notes. The air from the vent blew it out of my hand and onto the passenger seat. I grabbed it, turned down the air conditioning, and compared notes. As I suspected, the areas that Kevin said determined the last two elections were the ones written on my dad's note.

I started the car and drove into the God-awful evening traffic. All the roads going through Half-Way-Tree were like parking lots. It drove me crazy to be stuck with my thoughts and no way of figuring out a reason behind this strange coincidence.

I tried calling Sean, but it rang three times, then went to his voicemail. *"This is Sean, you know what to do."*

I thought about calling Peyton, but didn't know if she would be much help. So I just sat there, inching along in traffic. Thirty minutes later, I stopped at the intersection where I had followed Sean the other day.

Are you kidding me? I had looked down the road instinctively. To my surprise, Sean's car was there, large as life, parked in front of a taxi. I squinted to see if that was really his car, but I couldn't mistake the huge exhaust. Maybe it was my confused, overwhelmed state or the fact that I must be really insane that made me do it. When the light turned green, the cars ahead of me slowly moved off. I followed, fully intending to go home, but then the steering wheel turned left and I was parked behind the taxi.

I changed my shoes to some flats that I kept in the back. I reapplied my lip gloss, put my purse around my body, and walked towards the decorated fence. Even with the sun going down, the metal door was still hot to the touch. I pushed as hard as I did before, but no luck. It swayed a little and made a loud squeak, but did not open. A frightened, I'd-better-get-my-butt-out-of-here realization came over me, so I turned to walk away. As I did, the gate made a screeching sound and swung open. The big black guy with the security shirt stood in front of me. "Yes?"

"Hi! Remember me from the other day?" I said, trying to make light of my frantic state. He looked a little puzzled as he obviously did not know who I was.

"I work with Sean." I was going to add that I was the girl who came here in her house clothes, looking homeless. Before I could say that, he spoke.

"Oh, Tameka! Of course I remember you. You looking good—I hardly recognize you." He looked me up and down and up again. "Not that you didn't look good before, but now, wow!"

I felt grossed-out, but tried to keep my face agreeable.

He continued, "You know, I was just asking Sean for you when he came in.

"Oh, you were?" I asked, frightened.

"Yeah, he was telling me that he left you at the office, but he didn't tell me you were coming."

"I know. I finished up early so I decided to swing by," I lied, though not technically. I did finish early and I did swing by.

"Well, he can use all the help he can get. From what I hear, it's a big story he is working on," he said.

I absolutely did not know what he was talking about, but I nodded my head and agreed, "Yes, that is true. This one is huge."

He stepped aside to let me in. "You should find him same place," he told me.

I didn't know what same place he meant, as I had glimpsed Sean in the corridor last time. Before embarking on the long, winding stair underground, I turned. "You know what? I didn't pay attention the last time I was here. Where exactly should I walk?"

"It's easy to find, walk straight past the bar and turn left at the second corridor, then he should be in Neily's office on the right. You can't miss it."

I couldn't help asking, "Neily Ram, right?"

He seemed amused. "Yes, Neily Ram, which other Neily you know?"

"Long day," I said to him as I smiled and started the descent.

My smile quickly disappeared. The name Neily Ram ran through my head. I'd encountered another name listed on my dad's to-do paper. My legs started to wobble and the heat from my nerves grew more suffocating with each step toward the bottom of the stairs. I could hear the loud music and smell the mixed smoke from the weed and cigarettes.

I walked casually past the bar where the men were, once again, playing a serious domino game. The clanks from the dominoes made me jump each time. It was not as packed as it was before. A light-skinned girl with jet black hair and heavy makeup, wearing a hat and spandex dress, stared at me as she drank a beer by the bar.

I faced forward, walking quickly to the first corridor. When I got there, I looked in both directions. The corridor was empty and the sound from behind began to fade. The eerie, ominous feeling that I felt the last time came back.

I ran across the corridor and hid in the first wall pocket. I looked up and noticed hand-carved drawings overhead; I was not the first person to hide here. I bet this place was once used for something completely different. I wondered how the cavities or pockets in the walls came about. Whatever it was, I was just grateful for a place to hide.

I heard the tapping sounds in the distance. I still had to reach the next corridor where Sean and Neily Ram were supposedly meeting. I leaned closer to the wall and tried to talk to my crazy self. *So why exactly are you here? What happens if you do see Sean and Neily? What if Neily throws you out for trespassing or worse.* Before my mind got to worse, I snapped myself out of it.

With a quick scan of the hallway, I cautiously stepped out. Once in the open, I moved briskly, making my way to the second corridor. I could only make a left or go straight to the end of the hallway. To the left, where Sean and Neily should be meeting seemed like some offices. The doors were all closed.

As I contemplated what to do next, straight ahead, the tapping sound came back. In that direction, I could only see those iron bars, that looked like cells. Without thought, I started towards the sound. I came to the first set of bars and, true to my suspicion, it really was a jail cell. It had a little bed with no sheets and an old toilet in the corner. It was empty, as were the second and third cells. The tapping persisted, bringing me to the fourth cell, where a man sat on a chair with his back turned to me. I wasn't sure what he was doing, but he was clearly locked up and for a long time, based on his dirty white shirt, which draped his body like a curtain. The tapping sounds came from this cell.

I looked to my left to make sure there was no one coming. I was so nervous and scared that I started to walk backwards, but, before I could get out of sight, the tapping stopped and the man turned around, looking straight at me.

His salt and pepper hair was knotted and out. His beard needed grooming; it was long and short in different areas. He reminded me of a mad scientist. His expression was flat and he looked away from me for a moment. I froze, my mind blank.

Then he spoke, chuckling a little as he did. "How did you get back here?" He turned slightly to the side, half looking in my direction while still paying attention to what he was doing. He began mumbling, so I leaned in closer to the cell to hear what he was saying. Yet I still couldn't make out a thing.

"Hi, I'm Morgan."

He continued talking to himself in a low voice. I started to speak again, but he put his palm up, signaling for me to stop talking. I waited while he turned and started tapping away again. After a short while, he turned to faced me.

"Sorry, I had to finish my thought."

I was a bit confused, but, as he got to his feet, I could see an old typewriter on the ledge next to his chair. My dad came to mind when I saw the typewriter; he was the only other person I knew who had a typewriter. As the man moved, I could see a bunch of papers all over the floor. Although he was dirty and clearly been in here for a while, his face looked pleasant and trusting. I bet he would clean up nicely.

"Where am I?" I asked him, certain my face showed my fear.

He chuckled again, more visibly this time. "You come to my dungeon, free as a bird in the sky and ask me where you are? Little girl, I would advise you to walk quickly back in the direction you came from before the wrong people see you."

He made it back to his chair and I checked the area again to see if anyone was coming. I was not sure why; I could just turn around and leave, but my legs would not cooperate.

"What are you typing?" I asked, suddenly curious.

"Nothing to concern you—or anyone else, for that matter," he said. "I just write what's in my head, you know?"

I thought of my dad again, this time because I spotted a big black and white sticker on the man's typewriter. My dad's typewriter had a black and white sticker with the word Swoosh on it. I remember putting it there when Roxann gave him a pair of Nikes. He had placed it on my cheek, then I took it off and stuck it to his typewriter. It had stayed there.

The man was typing again as if I weren't even there. I was really about to leave, but I had to know.

"Does that sticker say Swoosh?"

He looked at the sticker and I heard him say, "Swoosh" quietly, but without directly answering me.

215

Then he turned fully and rolled his chair to the cell bars where I stood. His demeanor changed from pleasant to frightening and his voice changed from the nonchalant, sarcastic tone he had taken before.

"What are you really doing down here?" he asked.

"Not sure," I said. "I stumbled on this place once before and I had unanswered questions, so I came back."

"You stumbled?" he asked, a concerned look on his face.

Hearing my reason for being down here scared even me, so I tried to give him a better explanation.

"I mean, it's a long story. I saw a friend of mine come in and I followed him to see why he was here. Before I could find out, I saw these cells and heard the tapping sound and was curious, I guess."

He still clearly thought I was crazy, but he pushed past it and asked me, "Why would your friend be down here?"

"That's what I wanted to find out. I talked to the security guy out front, so I know he's meeting with Neily Ram."

"You spoke to the security at the front," he asked, perplexed.

"You see my friend works at a magazine and I don't know for sure, but I think he is doing a story. I also kind of told the guard that we are working on it together."

He sighed. "This is no place for you or your friend; you need to find your way out."

As soon as he said that, I heard footsteps and voices in the distance. We both froze, then he signaled for me to go in the direction of the last cell, the one next to him. I moved as fast as I could and, as I passed the fifth cell, also empty, I was relieved to find a wall pocket. I bent low and tucked myself all the way back out of sight, holding my heart within my chest.

A few seconds later, the footsteps grew louder, then stopped. I heard keys, then a loud squeaking sound as the heavy cell door slid open. There seemed to be more than one person. I heard laughter and what sounded like playful banter. Moments later, the loud cell door closed and the footsteps grew faint as the people walked away.

I sat still for a moment longer, then I snuck my head out to assess the area. It was all quiet again, so I walked back to my new friend's cell. He had his face in his plate, gobbling down what looked like corn beef and rice.

"Dinner time?" I asked lightheartedly.

"You want some?" he joked.

"I'm fine, thanks."

I stood there with my hands folded, watching him eat quickly. He slowed down and looked up. His face pleasant again, he said, "You better get out of here before you really get caught."

"Okay, you're right. I have no business being down here. But one question before I leave…"

He pushed his plate to the side and turned to face me fully. I hesitated, suddenly shy now that I had his

217

full attention. He raised his eyebrows, encouraging me to continue.

"What are you doing down here? I mean, why are you locked up?"

He thought for a minute, then he stood up and walked over to me.

"You see, some things are just how they are; you can't always save the world. The world don't want to be saved or changed. If you cannot comply, you sometimes get killed or, in my case, put away. Sometimes what you know can hurt you more than what you don't know. I'm doing my time and I'm okay with it. I am here because of a choice that I make every day to keep my family safe.

"Now you get on out of here safely and don't come back. These people are ruthless and who knows what they would do with a pretty little thing like you."

Just hearing that, I had a sudden sick feeling in my stomach. I'm sure he saw the grimace on my face.

He said, "Don't worry yourself, just get out the same way you came in."

As I turned to leave, he stepped away, saying, "One more thing."

I stopped and waited until he came back with a sealed envelope. He handed it to me and asked, "Could you please put a stamp on this and mail it?"

"What is it?" I asked.

"It's just a letter I've been meaning to send off. I usually ask Errol to mail things for me, but when he came by with the dinner another person was with him. I didn't want to get him in trouble for doing this for me."

I took the envelope, sliding it in my purse. I looked at him one more time and he nodded gratefully.

"Before I leave, can you at least tell me your name?"

"The name is Lance."

"Well, I'll see around Lance."

"Or not," he replied.

"One last thing—I promise. How do you have a typewriter down here?"

"They let me use it, since I am not allowed to have a computer," he said with a smirk.

And then he said it, what I had only ever heard Roxann say.

"You be careful, you and your friend; this is no country for young fools."

Chapter 15

Peyton spent the night after she left Oasis. I had worked in Roxann's store the evening before and was too tired to go to church with her. We stayed up most of the night as I filled her in on my week. I told her about Sean again at that underground location and how I met the prisoner, Lance. I told her about the letter that Lance gave me to mail.

"What was in the letter?" she asked.

"I don't know. I still have it; I was planning to mail it tomorrow."

"Morgan, let me see," she said, jumping off the bed.

"Why do you want it? It's sealed."

"Just let me see it," she insisted.

"It in my top left desk drawer."

She rumbled through my drawer, then she emerged with two letters in her hand.

"Which one is it?" she asked.

At first, I wasn't sure what she meant, then, when she brought them by the bed, I realized that one letter was the one from Lance and the other the one that my dad sent the other day. I had not planned to read it, so

I quickly pulled it from Peyton and returned it to the top drawer.

"What's that all about?" she asked.

"Nothing. That is nothing that I wish to read," I said.

She decided not to push, focusing on Lance's letter instead. It was made out to a Jodie Hall with an address in Kingston. Peyton had the look on her face that meant she was up to no good. My mouth still fell open as she pushed her fingers under the flap and opened Lance's letter.

"Peyton, you can't do that!" I lunged towards her where she sat at the foot of my bed, trying to get the letter from her.

"I just did," she said, laughing and escaping to my desk. She started reading it.

My sweetest Jodie,

I hope you and your mom are okay. It has been a few months since you saw me last, but you will see me soon, I promise. I need you to know that because of this job, I just cannot get away yet. I know that there are things that I cannot and will not be able to explain about the way that I left, but please know that I love you. Your mom is not happy with me now and I can't blame her. Tell her that I am sorry and I hope she will find it in her heart to forgive me. I missed your birthday last month, but I will make it up to you. My little

*girl is ten now! How proud I am of you. I think
of you every day and I hope you still think of me.
Take care of yourself and be strong. Remember
that you are always in your daddy's heart.*

Love you always and forever,
Daddy

"Oh wow, Peyton, he has a daughter. I wonder where she thinks he is?"

"Well, it said it right there in the letter," Peyton pointed out. "He said he was away at work. Why wouldn't he just tell her he got in trouble or, better yet, locked up?"

"I guess no one wants to tell their child that they are in jail," I replied.

"I wonder if the mother knows where he really is?" asked Peyton.

"I don't know. That place was creepy. I'm not even sure if it's a legal jail."

We were about to seal back the letter with a tape, but something about the letter seemed oddly familiar. I thought I might know why. When Peyton went to the bathroom, I dug into my Cinderella box, where I kept the few letters that my dad had sent me throughout the years. At the bottom, I found the very first one, which read:

My darling Morgan,

It has been a few months since you saw me last, but you will see me soon, I promise. I need you to know that I am working through a few things and, with this story I am working on, I just cannot get away yet. I know that there are things that I cannot and will not be able to explain about the way that I left, but please know that I love you. Your mom and brother are not happy with me, but I know that I can count on you to not give up on me. I hope one day you all will find it in your hearts to forgive me. I missed your birthday the other day, but I will make it up to you. My little girl is growing up. How proud I am of you. I think of you every day and I hope you still think of me. Take care of yourself and be strong. Remember that you are always in Daddy's heart.

Love you always and forever,
Daddy

I started comparing the letters side by side. The words were so much alike. I remembered how I felt receiving this letter. I had been confused, not knowing what I had done to cause him to leave. I had been disappointed that something had been more important in his life than his family. I had felt a helpless and sad sensation in the pit of my stomach, the one I knew Lance's little daughter would feel as well.

Before I could finish comparing the similarities, I heard Peyton coming out the bathroom. I quickly put Lance's letter on my printer and hit copy. Then I put it back in the envelope, sealed it with tape, and dropped it in my bag to mail the next day.

My mind felt jumbled and incapable of making sense out of the letters, so I lay on the bed. Peyton lay down next to me and, before we fell asleep, she must have noticed that I was lost in thought.

"So what's the deal with you and Sean?"

Grateful that she had clearly missed the mark on my thoughts, I went along with the change and rebelled.

"There is no deal!"

"No, something is up," she went on. "You have never done anything this reckless. You keep following this guy to this dangerous place without reason."

She turned to face me, smirking away while I stared at the ceiling, trying not to give her any evidence for her accusation. She saw that I wouldn't budge, so she shook my shoulders, making me face her.

"Would you please stop?" I yelled, hitting her with my pillow.

She grabbed the pillow. "I think someone is in love."

"I am not!"

She laughed and lay back on the bed. For a moment, neither of us said anything and then I did.

"I don't know what my deal with him is or if there is a deal. All I know is that I think about him all the time and I want to know more. And then I wonder why. I don't think I have the capacity to get close to people—you know how hard it is for me to have friends, much less a man. It doesn't matter, anyway. I'm sure he doesn't even think about me when I am gone."

"Of course he does. I watch him around you and he is very attentive," she said, grinning. Another moment passed, then she said, "That's nice, though, Morgan, really nice."

The week ended before I knew it. Saturday came and, although I planned to treat it like any other Saturday, I couldn't. While putting away my laundry, I had to listen to Peyton's annoying pleads.

"Come on, Morgan, it's your eighteenth birthday."

"I really don't see why we have to make a fuss. Today is just another day," I protested.

I was deep in my closet hanging up clothes while she played on my computer, trying to find the perfect place for us to go.

"This is it!" she would say and then, "No, not there. You know where we should go Morgan?"

I didn't answer because, knowing Peyton, she would tell me anyway. She continued like I knew she would and said, as if it was final, "We're going to Quad!"

"Quad? Why would I go somewhere with a bunch of sweaty people drinking and rubbing all over me? No, thank you."

"Come on, Morgan, you only turn eighteen once—plus you've never been clubbing before. It's a rite of passage into adulthood."

"Well, I don't think I am interested in every experience. I am okay living vicariously through others for some things. Plus, how many times have you gone clubbing? And all three times, didn't you come back with a horror story?"

She started to laugh. "That is not the point."

"Yes, it is! Need I remind you of the guy who burned you with his cigarette and gave you that permanent scar on your right arm? Or maybe the drunken guy who broke the glass that cut your toe? Should I continue?"

"Oh my God, you still remember that?"

"Yes, I do, so no thank you to Quad! I'm actually fine with just relaxing tonight. As I told you last night, I had a very busy week."

"So, what do you want to do? I've already invited the crew from church last night," she said.

"You invited people from church to a club?"

"Okay, I got your point, Morgan—it's a bad idea. I didn't invite them clubbing. I simply told them to clear their schedules because we are celebrating your birthday today."

She kept researching places on the computer, then she said, "What about that Japanese restaurant that we read about? The one with the great reviews that over-looks all of Kingston?"

I didn't answer, but that didn't stop her. "I can make a reservation and we can have a nice dinner."

I made a skeptical face, but I contemplated it for a bit. Before I conceded, I asked, "Who did you invite anyway?"

She mentioned her crew, redbone Eric, Bones, Lamb. I guess my face had a hint of my disappoint-ment at not hearing Sean's name because she quickly interjected, "I would have invited your boyfriend, but he wasn't there last night, either."

"That's alright. He probably wouldn't have come anyway—and he's not my boyfriend!"

"Almost missed that, didn't you?" she said with a grin.

My seat belt hugged my body as Peyton embarked on the curvy Stony Hill Road. The higher we went, the narrower the road. I kept praying to God that we wouldn't fall off the precipice.

We were running a little behind for our eight-thirty reservation at Majestic Sushi and Grill. Roxann and my Aunt Grace were already there, waiting for us to be seated.

Peyton stopped abruptly, squeezing her car close to the rock on my side of the road to make way for a truck coming around the corner. The truck's horn echoed loudly before it even came in sight. I really wished we hadn't taken this drive at night. The truck passed, making Peyton's car vibrate. Unbothered, she drove for five more minutes until we saw a wooden arrow pointing to Majestic.

Peyton said excitedly, "We made it in one piece!"

She pulled my hand away from my eyes; I was still unnerved by the drive. She went through the gate and parked on the grass in front of some coconut trees. She unbuckled her seat belt and then mine, which was slow to come off.

"Loosen up, it's your birthday! I have a full night planned. I hope you brought your dancing shoes," she said, bopping her head from side to side in the car and trying to make me smile. "You are now legal to drink and we are beautiful. I must say, you look rather hot tonight, Morgan!"

That made me laugh; just hearing that from Peyton sounded odd. I did look a bit edgier that my norm. I wore a fitted black and silver minidress that hit a few inches above my knees with a deep v-cut neckline.

As we walked to the steps leading to the restaurant, I tried pulling it up to hide my cleavage, which, in turn, made my dress even shorter. *This is what I get for letting Peyton pick my clothes.* I also wore a sparkly black strappy sandal, but at least I'd brought some silver flats in my bag; I was sure I would use them as the night progressed.

Peyton had spent most of the afternoon doing my makeup and straightening my hair. The layered cut that

I'd finally agreed to paid off. The front had short bangs and the layers extended gradually until my hair touched my upper back. With my smoky eyes and deep red lipstick, I looked nothing like my usual self. I was sure no one would recognize me.

Peyton wore a fitted red chiffon minidress cut low in the back with gold accessories. She had her hair pulled up in a ponytail and her face would be the envy of any paint swatch. Her lips were bright red with a deeper red on her cheeks. Her eyes sparkled from the gold glitter all over her eyelids.

I smiled. "You are on fire, Peyton!"

The hostess pulled open the heavy glass door for us and we walked in. The restaurant was beautiful. We passed an indoor waterfall at the restaurant's entrance, admiring the full-length yellow drapes that shimmered in the light from the candles on the table. We met up with the others seated on the white couch in the waiting area. I thought only Roxann and Aunt Grace were there waiting, but so was Bones, redbone Eric, and his sister Jackie, who sometimes came to Oasis, too.

"What a pleasant surprise," I said as I hugged them.

They all expressed awe of my appearance. Roxann just smiled as my aunt marveled about my new look. Roxann was always trying to add more color to my face or edge to my clothes, so I knew my over-the-top attire pleased her.

The hostess seated us at a big table next to the window. I glanced out at the spectacular view as the lights from Kingston illuminated the skies. I smiled; nothing was better to me than a great view.

"Isn't it beautiful, Morgan?" Peyton asked, following my gaze.

"It sure is," I said, giving her a big smile.

Roxann told my Aunt Grace that this would be a perfect location for any future event for her store. Peyton, busy talking to Eric and the others, didn't see as Tony came into the restaurant. He looked very nice in dark pants and a long-sleeved grey shirt. Next to him walked a beautiful Asian girl in a shiny grey dress. I watched Peyton's face as she spotted them. I saw the sudden surprise on her face, followed by her signature 'I don't care' act. She kept talking to the others.

Tony introduced Sarah to the group, then she came over to hug me and wish me a happy birthday. I could feel eyes on me as she did this, first Peyton's and then Roxann's. Roxann always wants to meet the girls Tony sees, but never gets the chance. I saw her at the other end, smiling and talking low to my aunt. Tony and Sarah sat down next to me.

As Tony studied the drink menu, his hand looked so much like my dad's that I couldn't help thinking of my father. I wondered for a moment what he must be doing. Probably living his life with his new family as usual and not giving a thought to today, his daughter's eighteenth birthday. As I thought that, a heavy cloud settled over me that I found very hard to shake.

The waiter came by and Tony announced, "This is my sister's eighteenth birthday; please fix her up with something spirited to drink."

Everyone agreed, shouting out drinks that I should get. I played it safe and asked for a glass of champagne.

Tony said, "Alright then, she wants to keep it classy. Bring us two bottles, please."

"Yes, maybe that will loosen her up," said Peyton.

She suddenly remembered that she was supposed to be acting like she didn't care. She glanced at Tony, then went back to her conversation with Eric and the others. We ordered sushi rolls and I ate only the cooked shrimp tempura and veggie ones. They were delicious and stuffed with ripe plantains. Peyton and Tony's friend Sarah both eagerly ate the raw tuna and salmon sushi rolls; clearly they had a lot in common. Roxann and I cringed at the sight, but Tony seemed to enjoy their ravenous energy.

After dinner, my gloomy feeling lingered. I smiled and seemed happy, but inside I felt really sad. When our plates were cleared, Roxann gave a beautiful toast.

"Morgan, I wish you all the joy today on this, your eighteenth birthday. This is your entrance into adulthood, even though you've been grown for years. You are always so responsible; I don't know where you get it from, certainly not Tony…"

Everyone laughed.

"I wish you all the success in your future endeavors and I am proud of you. I don't talk about him much, but I know that your dad would be proud of you, too."

My tears were about to fall and I willed them back in. To my relief, the servers came out singing and holding a beautiful double chocolate fudge birthday cake. I quickly wiped my eyes and blew out the candles. The three glasses of champagne that Tony and Peyton had tag-team poured for me were kicking in. I felt a bit more relaxed and relieved to be shaking off the funky mood that I was in.

At the front of the room, music started playing and the DJ asked people to come up and dance. It was ten-thirty, so Roxann got up to bid her goodbyes.

"It's time for us old people to get home," she announced.

Knowing Roxann, she just wanted to get down that crazy hill before it got any later.

"You guys stay and enjoy yourselves. Tony keep an eye on Morgan because it look like unu get mi pickney drunk."

"I am not drunk," I protested.

"Of course not, dear," my aunt said as she hugged me goodbye. "You wouldn't allow that to happen."

"I wouldn't allow that to happen," joked Tony.

"I don't know about that," Aunt Grace said playfully, nudging him as she hugged him goodbye, too.

Roxann came over to hug Tony's friend Sarah and said, "It was nice meeting you. Don't be a stranger now,

I hope to see you again soon." As she started to leave, she couldn't help meddling. "Tony, maybe you can bring her to your Granny and Grandpa's fiftieth anniversary celebration coming up."

Tony rolled his eyes. "Mommy, I thought you were leaving. Besides, Sarah won't even be here."

Sarah turned to Roxann. "I'm sorry, Ms. Ellis, I'm afraid he's telling the truth. I live in New York and I'm actually going back on Monday."

"Wow, New York! Long distant relationships are tough," Roxann said.

"Oh, no," they both said at the same time.

Sarah smiled and Tony held his head. "Sarah is just my sistrin, nothing else."

Roxann's face rattled with disappointment while Peyton's lit with a smile.

Chapter 16

walked them outside, said my goodbyes, and stopped by the bathroom to freshen up. When I returned, everyone had left except for Tony and Sarah, who were still sitting at the table. I perused the darkened room, which now resembled Oasis on a Friday night. Peyton and Eric were on the dance floor with Bones and Eric's sister Jackie nearby, all bouncing to Farrell's 'Happy' song. As I approached the table, my phone screen lit up. I sat down to look at it; it was a text from Sean.

So how does it feel to be 18?

I smiled at the thought that he remembered. *It feels horrible.*

Where are you?

At a restaurant sitting.

Which restaurant?

Majestic—this sushi restaurant up Stony Hill.

*I know that restaurant, I love that restaurant.
You should go on the patio and see the view of
the city.*

I can already see it from where I am sitting.

*You need to go to the patio and walk all the way
to the end and look out from the balcony… The
view is like nothing you've ever seen.*

I needed a breather anyway, so I told Tony that I
was going out for some air. I passed the DJ booth and
stepped outside. Uniquely shaped orange and lime
green couches decorated the patio. The plush pillows,
fresh greenery, and big soft sky lanterns that hung from
the ceiling created a cozy, romantic feel. The night air
was cool and the lights from the city below lit up the sky.

My five-inch sandals had become unbearable to
walk in, so before walking to the end of the patio to
witness the never-before-seen views, I sat and changed
into my sandals. When I got up, another text came in
from Sean.

Why don't you ever wear comfortable shoes?

I was about to answer him when it dawned on me.
How does he know I changed my shoes?
As I continued down the patio I spotted a perfect
silhouette overlooking the balcony. He turned around
with a big grin on his face. He looked remarkable in

white slacks and a nicely pressed black shirt with silver buttons and rolled-up sleeves. The contour from his fresh haircut and shaved beard made his face the view I would never forget.

I'm not sure why his presence meant so much to me. Maybe it was just the surprise or the fact that I drank some champagne or maybe it was because I was in such a removed state. I felt like the girl at the end of a movie who thought the guy had gone until he showed up at the airport just before she boarded her flight. I couldn't move or muster up words to speak.

He walked slowly towards me, wrapped his arms tightly around me, and simply said, "Happy birthday."

The warmth of his body and the intoxicating smell of his cologne jolted me back into consciousness. He released his grip and took a step back. His eyes perused me up and down. I felt flushed. I couldn't read the expression on his face, but it seemed a mixture of good and bad.

"What is it?" I insisted.

"Oh nothing, you look lovely, just lovely."

I picked up on a hint of something in his voice, but I chose to ignore it.

"Come see," he said.

He took me to end of the balcony where he had been standing. In the breathtaking panoramic view, the lights brought the city right to us. Out in the distance, on top of the hill, we saw large houses already strung with dancing Christmas lights. We could feast our eyes on an immaculate, well-lit garden just below the balcony on the grounds of the restaurant. We rested our hands on the railing, witnessing the magnificent views, enjoying the silence that filled the night.

After a moment, Sean said, "I'm sorry I missed your dinner."

I smiled. "That's okay. You really didn't miss much. I wasn't there half the time anyway."

"Where were you?" He looked perplexed.

"I mean, I wasn't there in my mind," I said hesitantly.

He considered this for a moment, then asked, "Do you want to sit?"

"Sure." We walked over to the vibrantly colored couches and took a seat on one of the lime green ones.

Just then, the door slammed and I turned to see Peyton.

"Oh, there you are," she said with a smirk on her face.

As she sat down on the edge of the couch, she hugged me from behind and whispered, "I should have known. Happy birthday!" Then she said aloud, "So, Sean, you made it. For a moment there I thought you didn't get my message."

"Sorry, I had an interview for a story that ran over time."

"Yeah, yeah," she said, then continued with a big grin. "And then, of course, you had to go to your stylist and beautician so that you could look like this."

He smiled and glanced at me. I was enjoying their playful banter. He chuckled and said to her, "Well, the occasion called for nothing less. And you are ravishing as well."

"You are goo-oood," she said.

We all laughed.

Peyton got up from behind me and said, "Sean, do you dance?"

"I have a few moves," he joked.

"Well, I know Morgan doesn't dance, but I expect to see your moves on the dance floor before the night is over."

"For sure," he said.

She danced her way back inside and left us to our solitude.

"So you don't dance?"

"More like I can't and I haven't," I said jokingly.

"How do you know you can't if you haven't done it?" he asked.

"Of course you caught that."

We both laughed, trailing off into silence. Sean got up and pulled a nearby table towards us. He put his feet on the table and threw his head back on the couch. He smiled and signaled with his head for me to do the same.

"That's alright," I said.

"Come on," he insisted.

I just sat on my side of the couch with my hands wrapped around me for warmth in the cool night breeze.

Then he said, "You can't, can you?"

"I can't what?" I asked.

"You can't put your feet up."

"No, I just won't."

He tried egging me on. "You won't because you can't."

"Of course I can."

"Well, then prove me wrong."

I gazed at him and said, "Maybe I will."

I slowly put both feet on the table next to his.

"Now was that so hard?" he asked.

I was about to answer when he said, "Don't answer that."

I laughed.

He said, "So now that we are both comfortable, let's play Truth."

"No, we will not," I protested.

His head still back on the couch, he turned to face me. In a relaxed, easy tone, he asked, "Why not?"

"You know why. The last time we played that game you walked away mad and didn't talk to me for several weeks."

He faced forward, thinking. "Okay, you're right. But I apologized and that will not happen again."

He sounded sincere, so I relented. "Okay, fair enough. So who starts?"

"Well, you asked the last question, so it's my turn," he said.

"And you did not answer my last question, so it is still my turn," I quickly pointed out.

"Alright, alright," he conceded.

"Let's see…" I said, thinking of the perfect question. I suddenly remembered that he told Peyton that he was late because he was working on a story. "So what kept you working late today?"

"I've been working on a story that's supposed to showcase two groups finally getting along, even though I'm not so sure anymore," he said, trailing off.

"Why?" I asked.

He moved his feet off the table and assumed his familiar position, looking down at the ground before he began.

"Yesterday I saw something that changed things a little."

"What did you see?" I asked, suddenly even more curious.

"Um, a person that I recognized was in the wrong place."

He wasn't offering much, so I felt like I needed to pry for information.

"So the person being at the wrong place now makes you unsure of your story?" I asked.

Before he answered, he turned to face me. "You know, you've asked me, like, five different questions, right?"

I smiled. "What can I say? I'm making up for last time."

He proceeded to answer. "Yes, it makes me a little unsure. You know the way you felt when you were at the debate? The feeling that something was just not right?"

"Yeah," I answered.

"That's the same feeling that I have."

"You need to figure out what that is," I told him.

"That's the plan," he said.

He turned again, staring at me a little longer than usual. Then he said, "My turn."

"Okay," I said. "What do you want to know?"

"Where was your mind tonight?"

I looked at him, confused. *What is he talking about?*

He elaborated. "When I got here, you told me that you were not present in your mind at dinner."

"Oh, that. I did say that, didn't I? Well, I'm not sure entirely what it is. I know, though, that it has to do with my dad not being here. I mean, I'm fine every day. I accept that he doesn't want to be our lives anymore. But for some reason, whenever it's a special occasion, I think about him and I…"

I paused, trying to find the words, but then Sean finished for me. "You miss him."

"Yeah, I guess I do. I think I've been extra good for the last few years, in part because Tony has been so bad, but secretly in hopes that he would come back. And, somewhere along the line, I think I forgot to live."

"You look living to me," he joked.

I smiled back. "You know what I mean. I'm eighteen and I haven't done the mischievous things that people my age do."

"Like what?" he asked.

I knew I should not have answered, but I felt so open with Sean. It felt like I could tell him anything.

"For instance, tonight is the first time I've drunk alcohol."

"I don't see the problem there," he said. "The legal age for drinking alcohol is eighteen."

I shook my head. "You know what I mean."

"No, I don't," he said. "What else have you not done?"

"I have never been to a club, never stayed out until an obscene hour, never smoked, never took a weekend trip with friends, never skipped school...the list goes on and on."

He had a comical look on his face. He said, "Do you hear yourself? That's not you missing out on anything. Your life won't be impacted by not doing those things."

"I think so, but I'm not done. There's more," I said.

He held his head as I continued.

"I've never had a boyfriend or even kissed a guy before."

He laughed loudly when I said that.

"Now you are making fun of me. I'll just stop."

His laughter came to an abrupt halt. "No, no. I'm not making fun of you. It's just funny that you think you are missing out for not kissing a boy. Morgan, what you're describing is called staying out of trouble."

I wasn't looking at him, but I knew he searched my face to see if I understood.

"Yeah, I guess you are right," I said.

"And I promise you that, one day, you will meet the right person and you will be able to cross that off your list."

My stomach dropped suddenly. I smiled, trying to hide my disappointment that he was pawning me off to some random guy.

Just then the door opened again. The sound of Chronixx singing spilled out the door, blaring from the speakers, "*Smile, girl, smile, smile for me, Jamaica.*" Two girls and a guy came out on the patio, walking past us and down to the balcony. The smoke from their cigarettes filled the air, making it apparent why they were out here. Sean jumped to his feet and put his hand out to pull me up. As I stood up, I wrapped my arms around my shoulders shielding my body from the chilly night's air.

"I know something that you have never done that will not even reach your list," he said.

"What's that?" I asked.

"Come on; let's go inside," he said.

When we opened the door Chronixx was still singing and a lot more people were on the dance floor. Sean told me that he would be right back, so I looked around the dimmed room to see if I could find the others. Most of the tables were gone; only a few were set up at one side of the room. I spotted Tony's friend Sarah sitting by the bar area, so I walked over to her.

"Hey," I called out to her.

243

"There you are," she said. "Anthony was just asking Peyton for you."

I leaned close to her, since I had to speak loud over the music.

"I was outside on the patio, then I ran into a friend and was busy yapping."

Just then, the music changed from the lively sound of Chronixx to John Legend's slow ballad, "All of Me."

I could hear better then, so I asked Sarah, "Where is Tony?"

She pointed out on the dance floor and I searched in the direction that she pointed, then spotted him dancing with Peyton. They looked comfortable, like two people in love.

"Oh there he is ... dancing ... with Peyton. Well, would you look at that," I said, puzzled. I checked Sarah's reaction.

We sat there staring until she said, "He likes her, you know."

"He does? Did he tell you that?" I asked, trying to act surprised.

"Well, not in so many words, but, before her friend left, he couldn't take his eyes off her."

Her expression was hard to read. I couldn't help wondering if she was disappointed. I gave her a sympathetic look and she quickly picked up on it.

"Don't worry about me; we really are just friends. Peyton came over to ask me and Tony to dance and I

told him to go ahead. I knew he wanted to, a
she said, smiling.

I nodded and smiled back, then she said, "At on
point, there may have been something, but we got
over that—plus, I have a great guy back at home in
New York."

"Oh... good for you," I said.

"So, what about you?" she asked.

"What about me?" I asked, clearly missing her
question.

She elaborated. "Anyone special in your life?"

As I was about to answer no, Sean walked up.

"There you are," he said. "I went back to the patio
looking for you."

"Oh sorry, I was just talking to Tony's friend Sarah."

He put his hand out to shake hers, then introduced
himself. He had a jacket in his hand and said, "I brought
this for you."

I looked at Sarah. She raised her eyebrows, smiled,
and mouthed, "Good for you."

"We're inside now; I don't need it anymore. Thank
you, though," I argued.

He looked me up and down with the same mixed
expression he had outside. He put his oversized jacket
on me and said, "Yes, you do."

Then I realized that Sean's problem might be with
my outfit. I had never worn anything like it and he must
have found it too revealing. *Why does he care?* And
then, he broke that thought.

nd. "Are you ready to keep your
nger? Come on, dance with me."
don't dance."

ed and Peyton and Tony walked over
were standing.

ey, is that Sean the man?" Tony yelled as he and
Sean did their silly fist greeting before Tony sat by
Sarah. "So, that's where she was."

He nudged her. "Only Sean the man can get her
away for so long."

"Shut up, Tony," I said, annoyed.

"So, what's going on here?" he asked Sarah.

"Great entertainment, actually," Sarah said. "I'm
just watching to see if your sister can talk her way out
of dancing."

"Oh yes, go dance," Peyton said, pushing us away.

"I don't dance!"

"Come on, Morgan. It's your birthday; please go
dance," she begged. "You'll have fun. I'll even come
with you guys."

I looked at Sean with a flat, unhappy expression. He
said, "You don't have to if you can't dance."

"I can dance; I just don't."

"So now you can dance," he said, laughing. With his
intense stare and velvet tone he said, "I don't believe
you. Prove me wrong."

Peyton chimed in, "Yes, prove us wrong!"

They all stood looking at me.

"Okay, let's go," I said.

They started cheering.

As the calypso song, "Ragga, Ragga," started I let my guard down and pulled my hair up. I made my way onto the dance floor with Peyton and Sean. They both laughed and pointed to me, obviously impressed that I actually had moves.

After a few minutes, the DJ announced the last song of the night and the music changed to Boys II Men, "End of the Road."

Peyton leaned in to Sean and said, "You can handle this, right?"

She walked off the dance floor, leaving me with Sean, who stared at me with his piercing eyes and his mischievous smirk. He didn't give me the chance to talk my way out of it. Instead, he grabbed my waist and pulled me closer. I didn't argue. Wrapped in his oversized jacket, I rested my head on his shoulder and we danced.

When I finally said my goodbyes and got in the car, the clock flashed 1:32. I put my seat back and Sean laughed at my exhaustion. Between the champagne and the dancing my body wanted to shut down. Sean blew his horn at Peyton and Tony as he drove off. Tony had come to the party in Sarah's car, but she had called it a night at some point while we were dancing. So Peyton graciously offered to drop him at home, since she had to take me home anyway.

Then, when we got outside, Sean mentioned that he had something in his car for me, so Peyton had said, "Why don't you just take her home? We'll be right behind you guys."

We started down Stony Hill and, although the loud exhaust from Sean's car buzzed behind us, I didn't feel as scared as I did going up. I brought my seat back up and Sean asked if I was alright.

"I'm fine," I said. "Just tired—look at the time!"

He laughed. "This time isn't bad at all."

"Isn't bad? It's almost two!"

"Well, look at the bright side. You got some items crossed off your list tonight."

"I did? Like what?"

"For starters, you can't say you haven't stayed out late and you can't say you've never been to a club."

"I have not," I argued.

"In case you missed it, the restaurant turns into a club after eleven."

"That's what that was?" I asked, as clueless as ever.

He laughed at my naivety. "And you did a little something on the dance floor, so that does not even have to get on the list."

"That was not just a little. I threw down," I joked

"Okay, okay, let's not get carried away," he said. "You only danced to a few songs."

He slowed as we approached the bottom of the hill. The street was not too busy and, not far behind, I could see the lights from Peyton's car. We made a right, then stopped at the light.

Peyton pulled up next to us and shouted, "Why are you stopping?"

She then proceeded through the red light. Sean and I started laughing, though he stayed put, waiting for the light to change. While we waited, he reached into the back seat and pulled out a tiny gift bag.

"This is for you," he said.

The little bag was as lightweight as it looked; I felt sure that it was empty. Although he had said that he had something for me, it still surprised me. I didn't know how I felt about it.

I looked at him. "You got me something? What is it?"

I held the bag tightly in my lap, so tense that I must have resembled a statue.

"Aren't you going to open it?" he teased. "You know your birthday is over, right?"

"No, it's not. The entire month of December is mine," I joked back, happy to be on familiar footing again.

The red light turned green and Sean drove down the lonely road. I pulled the ribbon of the little bag and reached in. I pulled out a small, thin, nicely bound square booklet. The title was printed on the cover, *Morgan's 18th Birthday Wish List*.

I felt puzzled, confused, and a bit flattered before I even knew what was written in the book. The glossy paper, the whimsical script, the fact that he remembered my birthday long enough to create something with me in mind—it was overwhelming. I could feel tears welling up in my eyes and I was glad the night's darkness shielded my emotions.

"It's beautiful," I said, just over a whisper. I ran my fingers slowly over the embossed letters on the cover.

He laughed at my dramatic reaction. "You know the actual gift is inside, right?"

He turned onto my street and, shortly after, parked by the fountain at the front of my house. He turned on the light in the car. "So, are you going to look inside? I worked very hard on this, you know."

"I can see," I said as I opened the booklet.

It consisted of about ten thick, perforated pages.

He stopped me before I could read it and said, "Before you read it, there are rules."

"Rules?" I echoed.

"More like a requirement," he said in a fun tone.

"Okay…and what is that?"

"You have to embrace and at least attempt to fulfill the things on your wish list."

"Hmmm, I would agree, however… how do you know what to put on my wish list?"

"Trust me," he said, touching my hand and making a point to look in my eyes. "I know."

I felt something warm in my head and a quiver all the way to my spine; I had no fight left in me.

"I'll see about that," I finally said with a smile.

Number one—Bottomless grape soda from Oasis.

I laughed aloud as he peered over to see what I was reading. I read number two aloud, "*Unlimited help with final paper.* Hmmm, you know I will be taking you up on that."

However, number three really got me thinking— *Accompany me on a story that I am working on.* Number four read, *Free choice; anything that you wish.*

Numbers five through eight were handwritten, obviously late additions to his booklet. Five read, *Go on a weekend trip with your friends.* Six—*Sort things out with your dad.* Seven and eight would have my brain in knots for weeks to come. Seven—*Open your heart to finding the right guy* and eight—*Get that first kiss.*

I just sat there in his car for a moment. I didn't know what to say. This was by far the most thoughtful gift that I had ever received. I kept my emotions in check, though. I turned to him, smiled, and said, "Thank you. This is the most compact gift that I've ever received."

We both laughed.

He said, "And by compact, do you mean that you like it?"

"No, I mean that I love it," I said, giving him a big grin.

"I didn't know what to get you and I didn't want to ask, so I thought I would listen to what you are always whining about."

We laughed again.

"Ms. Logan did say you are known for your excellent listening skills," I joked. "So, when can I cash in?"

"It's open; you can cash in whenever you like. Of course, only for the things that I can help you with, I mean."

He reached over to where I was sitting, scanned the booklet, and said, "That looks like one through four; the others, I'm afraid you will have to figure out on your own."

My stomach dropped again, just like it did earlier. Once again, I covered it with a smile. He walked me to the door and hugged me goodbye. I hugged him back, letting go when I noticed that it was lasting a little longer than usual. He stepped back, smiled, and shook his head like he was having an inside joke with himself.

As he walked backward toward his buzzing car, he said, "I hope you enjoyed your birthday, Morgan. I'll see you around."

And just like that, my eighteenth birthday was over.

I wonder sometimes if God makes a clear delineation or chooses a point, then he says, "It is now time to grow up." At that moment, He says, "From here on out, childish matters are no longer for you. You've been coddled enough. Let me see what you can do."

I envision a big red button looming and in 5,4,3,2,1, it's pushed! And all of a sudden, expectations change and the course that you are on gets even harder. God stands in the distance saying, "Push through, stretch, you've been tested long enough to be able to handle the hurdles that are coming your way."

In bed that night, I thought of my dad again, as well as the events of the whole week. I took the letters out again and compared them. The words from the letter from Lance to his daughter were too familiar; some were the same exact words as the letter from my dad. Something didn't seem right and his typewriter... Why was his typewriter in the dungeon?

I couldn't make sense of it all, but a feeling over-took me. Things were not what they seemed. My dad is in trouble; I'm sure of it. He didn't want to leave, he had to. It's all making sense now. I have to help him!

I've since wondered if that was the moment when I turned 18. Was it when it was decided for my switch to be turned on? I lay there, still, with my imagination getting the best of me. I felt the revving, the prodding, the launching of something big. My heart raced with fear of the unknown and the discomfort of growing up, yet the adrenalin let me take a deep breath and say, "I'm ready; let's go!"

About the Author

Sidonie Walsh was born and raised in Jamaica and moved to the United States in her early teens. She has long loved the art of storytelling and dreamed of capturing the hearts and imaginations of others with exciting and inspirational stories about hope and love. The mystical beauty and rich  culture of her country inspired the setting for her debut novel. Sidonie's appreciation for her country led her to write The Natural Mystique- lure of the Caribbean in the Break Away Moments travel magazine.

She studied Public Relations and Journalism, and this is book one in the NCFYF two-part series. At work and in her spare time, she loves the thrill of a deal, negotiating and creating win-win relationships. Her hobbies include reading, writing, cooking and traveling. Sidonie lives between Florida and Virginia with her husband and three children. She strives to be a positive instrument of hope, searching within, and honoring her Lord and Savior, Jesus Christ, in her writings.

CPSIA information can be obtained
at www.ICGtesting.com
Printed in the USA
LVHW041046021219
639121LV00004B/333/P